THE
TRANSITIONER'S
HANDBOOK

GO NATURAL IN 5 EASY STEPS

Dr Lola Akingbola

BookVenture Publishing LLC
1000 Country Lane Ste 300
Ishpeming MI 49849
www.bookventure.com
Hotline: 1(877) 276-9751
Fax: 1(877) 864-1686

Ordering Information:
Quantity sales. Special discounts are available on quantity purchases by corporations, associations, and others. For details, contact the publisher at the address above.

Printed in the United States of America.

Library of Congress Control Number	2019933942
ISBN-13: Softcover	978-1-64348-887-5
Pdf	978-1-64348-888-2
ePub	978-1-64348-889-9
Kindle	978-1-64348-890-5

Rev. date: 02/11/2019

CONTENTS

INTRODUCTION.. ix

    HAIR STORY I – MY DECISION TO TRANSITION............................. X

    Is transitioning right for you?...xii

    Why are you transitioning? xiii

    Welcome to your transition!... xv

STEP 1

HOW LONG IS YOUR TRANSITION?....................................... 1

        Thinking of Relaxing your hair again? 2

    Dispelling the Myths #1: I have to wear an afro all the time!..... 2

    Choosing the length of your transition 3

    How will you mark reaching your goal? 4

    Getting to know your hair!.. 5

    Hair Science I: Hair Types.. 6

        Type 1 / Straight hair 6

        Type 2 / Wavy hair 6

        Type 3 / Curly hair... 7

        Type 4 / Coily to Kinky hair 7

    Does hair type matter?... 7

    Step 1 – Learning Points 10

    Step 1 - Action Plan... 11

STEP 2

HANDLING THE TWO TEXTURES!..12

    Dispelling the Myths #2: "your hair WILL break

    as you transition" 14

    Hair science II: Relaxers weaken the hair strand..............15

    First lesson: protect that demarcation line!....................... 16

    How to apply a protein TREATMENT? 18

    Hair Story II - My early transitioning months....................20

Two Very Different Textures..20

Handling the Demarcation Line..21

Detangling your transitioning hair......................................23

Suggested Protein treatments 24

Step 2 - Learning Points 26

Step 2 - Action Plan...26

STEP 3

GET A GOOD TRANSITIONING REGIMEN!..........................27

Dispelling the myth #3: "I can't go natural, it's too
expensive!"...27

Build your transitioning routine - Three parts...................28

1. Washing transitioning hair..29

2. Deep conditioning For transitioners...........................34

    Hair Science III: Why does natural hair get so dry? 34

3. Daily Moisturizing for Transitioners...........................37

    A. The WET-SET Method..37

    B. The Spray AND GO Method.....................................38

    C. The L.O.C. Method 39

How your moisture routine fits into daily life? 40

Recommended Hair Cleansers 40

Recommended Conditioners...40

D-I-Y Deep Conditioning Recipes.......................................41

Step 3 - Learning Points 43

Step 3 - Action Plan...43

STEP 4

STYLE IT - LIKE A PRO!..44

Protective Styles...45

Low-manipulation Styles 47

Hair Science: Why is curly/kinky hair so prone to breakage?..47

Choosing your transitioning style 48

Protective Styling Manual...50

Edge (Hairline) Control 51

Bunning 101...53

Parting your Hair 65

Parting Types..67

Styling with Braids..68

Using Extensions in your Hair..80

    Twisting with Extensions | How-To 84

Tips for caring for Protective Styles.....................................86
Low-Manipulation Styles...88
Hair Science: The Bonds in each hair strand 89
Tips for caring for Low-Manipulation Styles 103
Step 4 - Learning Points 103
Step 4 - Action Plan... 104

STEP 5

THE BIG CHOP- ALL'S WELL THAT ENDS WELL.................... 105
Dispelling the Myths #5: Going Natural will end all
hair WOES! 106
Trimming Transitioning Hair 107
How-to | Trimming Transitioning hair.............................. 109
The Big Chop – Making it happen...................................... 111
    Salon or at home?... 111
The Big Day 113
The Big Reveal!... 113
Go Natural but don't break the Bank! 115
    Trying Out New Products – the triple test...................... 116
    Transition without breaking the Bank!.......................... 117
Step 5 - Learning Points 117
Step 5 – Action Plan... 118

BONUS STEP 6

TRANSITIONING FOR THE PROFESSIONAL 119
Your Hair and the Workplace.. 119
Transitioning for Children 121
Tips for Styling and Time Management with Children 122
My Top Three Child-friendly YouTube Hair Channels.............. 123
Children's Hair Book Resources 123
Step 6 - Learning Points 123
Step 6 – Action Plan... 124

APPENDIX.. 125
Hair Care Glossary of Terms... 125

INTRODUCTION

*"THERE'S MORE TO LIFE THAN HAIR BUT
IT'S A GOOD PLACE TO START"*

The Aussie Philosophy © 2013 Procter & Gamble

When I embarked on my healthy hair journey in July 2008, I planned to achieve healthier - and hopefully, longer - hair. If you had met me at this point, you would have heard me say that I was "happy with my relaxer". Yet if you then told me that within two years I would decide to go natural, I would either have laughed or rolled my eyes. You see, *relaxed hair was all I had ever known.*

After all, my first relaxer was applied at the tender age of 6! I had grown up with a relaxer. My mother had relaxed hair as did most of my aunts and cousins. Notably, I did encounter a few family members who briefly deviated to a Jheri-curl (when it was the "in"-style). From this background, I didn't see how I could possibly embrace any other hairstyle? You can only imagine my current (happy) surprise at wearing my natural kinks and coils!

....

'RELAXED HAIR WAS ALL I HAD EVER KNOWN!'

....

As my journey progressed, I began to realise certain things about myself, which I had previously (subconsciously) ignored.

1. **I preferred having thicker hair:** I discovered this after I started to texlax my hair – leave relaxer on my new growth for only

7 – 12 minutes and thereby UNDER-PROCESS on purpose. I liked the semblance of a curl pattern this technique left behind;

2. **I didn't mind my shrinkage**: simply, this was the way my curly new growth made my hair seem shorter than it really was as I got closer to next relaxing day. I was comfortable with knowing - and not always showing - my true hair length;

3. **I was always (secretly) dreading the next relaxer process:** I was applying my own relaxer processes for the last year before my transition and I trusted my technique.

Nonetheless, I feared that I might over-process the new growth and end up with straighter roots than the hair below it. A variation on a natural-haired lady's accidental relaxer nightmare!

HAIR STORY I – MY DECISION TO TRANSITION

With these recurring thoughts, my decision was made by the end of January 2010. I was going to discover exactly what my natural hair looked like. I had been reading and researching this over the Christmas period. I was fairly convinced that *THIS – going natural -* was my next challenge.

Definition:
Going Natural: *the decision or process of growing out your natural hair whether from previous chemical processes or heat-induced damage to your natural texture. This can either involve 'transitioning' (see below) or an immediate 'big chop'.*

At that point, I reasoned that since I would eventually cut off the relaxed ends, I would be less devastated if I got the new growth or natural roots to a "practical" length beforehand.

Then, my hair had grown to reach the middle of my back. I knew with absolute certainty that I would not have the courage to cut off waist-length hair if I waited for waist-length hair before going natural!

There was also no doubt that I would get some very worried looks - and shady comments - from family members if I even *CONSIDERED* cutting off all of my hair. The utmost reason was, I was now very reluctant to let it go of the longer, thicker hair I had worked so hard for in the preceding 2 years! Hence, I decided to *TRANSITION*.

Definition
Transitioning: *THE PROCESS OF GROWING OUT RELAXERS, TEXTURIZERS OR OTHER CHEMICAL PROCESSES TO ALLOW ONE TO HAVE NATURAL HAIR AT AN EASILY-STYLED LENGTH WHEN THE CHEMICALLY-TREATED ENDS ARE EVENTUALLY REMOVED*

This is simply the time between your current hair styling technique and your ultimate goal hair style – whether it's in loose curls and kinks or in newly-formed locs. In this book, I will discuss growing out chemical styles to reveal your loose natural hair pattern. Transitioning was the perfect option for me.

So I announced my decision online - on the hair forums that I frequented - and this was met with encouragement and advice. My next step was to learn about this new "transitioning" step before things became too tricky.

At the end of my transition, my hair had reached hip length at the beginning of August 2012. I had initially reached hip-length at the start of May 2012 and then cut two inches off the ends. I reasoned that with proper care, I would regain that couple of inches in time for my holiday (and thankfully, I was right!). Secondly, I was starting to *finally* feel ready to part with my relaxed ends.

Below are pictures showing my hair length at the end of my transition just before my *big-chop*.

Definition
Big chop: *the final hair cut that removes any remaining chemically-treated or damaged ends of hair, leaving only your natural, virgin hair.*

FIGURE 1: MY HAIR LENGTH AT THE END OF MY TRANSITION!

IS TRANSITIONING RIGHT FOR YOU?

Looking at the pictures above, you might assume that transitioning is the best thing since sliced bread. You may even think it's quite an easy thing to do. However, like many worthwhile pursuits in life, it was an uphill struggle - especially at the start. Many women (mostly hair care professionals) will actively try to convince you that you *cannot* grow out a chemical process without significant breaking of the hair. They will tell you that you need a drastic haircut – like shaving the head bald! I did not believe this. So I went online and searched for women who had done just the opposite - to prove them wrong.

....

'MANY HAIR CARE PROFESSIONALS WILL TELL
YOU THAT YOU NEED A DRASTIC HAIRCUT.'

....

On YouTube, Hairlista.com and Keepitsimplesista.ning.com, I found many examples showing that it could be done. Furthermore, on Fotki, a picture posting site, I found other women who had successfully grown out their relaxers over at least 2 years and achieved great lengths without scary **breakage.**

<u>*Definition*</u>
Breakage: *this is when hair breaks off at points of weakness in the strand. When transitioning, this is most commonly seen between the new growth and the chemically-processed ends. However, it also commonly occurs at the ends of the hair strand if when these are mishandled.*

I made a quick study of these women and their respective hair care regimes and noted down the similarities. I plan to share these steps with you because they helped me experience a much smoother transitioning period. I also read a few books before finally deciding on my natural regimen. Before I knew it, my natural hair (new growth) was longer than my relaxed length (with gentle trims along the way). The added bonus of transitioning was that I could glimpse my hair's growth potential – beyond hip-length.

The first thing to clarify is your reason for starting this transitioning journey.

WHY ARE YOU TRANSITIONING?

Before acting on such a momentous decision, it is crucial to establish why you are doing it.

Is it to grow out a relaxer or heat-damaged hair? Is it to change things up? I knew a lady who transitioned with the plan to eventually relax it again. This time, she wanted to leave some texture in the hair – a Texlax – and thereby, enjoy thicker hair from the under-processing. She went natural simply to get a nice clean slate to start from.

Are you doing this because someone said you would be a pretty natural? Or is it to impress someone? Are you doing it to prove something to that nay-sayer? Or are you following the crowd of new naturals springing up all over?

I will be honest with you: any reason for transitioning that is outside of your personal choice will lead to a harder or failed transition. What do I mean? Well, if you are doing this to get favour in someone else's eyes, you will find it hard to keep going in their absence or, even worse, if they voice their disapproval.

My mother has been on a parallel journey with me, struggling to understand why I would supposedly "hide" my hair length in my natural hair pattern and refuse to relax it. She wondered why I was styling my own hair and refusing to use heated hair tools to straighten it. She almost seemed to be taking my decision to go natural as a personal attack on her!

Guess what? She is now the biggest natural hair PR/ spokeswoman! She loves it and tells everyone she meets about me. This was not an overnight transformation, mind. It took over 2 years - almost my entire transitioning time!

....

'ANY REASON OUTSIDE YOURSELF WILL LEAD
TO A HARDER OR FAILED TRANSITION.'

....

Secondly, if you are expecting to have hair that looks like someone else's – say, your sister's – you may be in for quite a shock! Within the same family and even on the same head of hair, there can be very different curl patterns. Expecting loose curls and getting kinky hair could be your ultimate stumbling block! Conversely, expecting thicker hair and finding your hair strands are still quite fine (individually) may leave you disheartened.

I have three brothers - no sisters - so I had nothing to guess from. After all, they had never grown their hair past either a buzz cut or very small afros – the latter when saving up between barbershop visits. My mother was the original relaxer-user in the family. Hence, I had *no idea what to expect*. Knowing this, I decided to enjoy whatever hair I grew and just be thankful that it did grow.

Now I would be lying if I said I didn't want my hair to look thicker in twisted styles like some heads of hair that regularly accosted my eyes on YouTube! I wanted that! However, I had to remember that this was going to be a unique journey and I was trying to listen to my hair (I'll explain this later on) and grow that hair! I joined groups on hair forums such as "No Big-Chop for me" and "Transitioners' support threads" and found sisterhood.

Just for fun, here are some questions you may have already encountered (or soon will) after announcing your decision to go natural:

Why did you do that?
Oh wow! Are you getting dreads?
Can I touch it?
How do you wash it?
Are you sure you're not just going through a phase?

WELCOME TO YOUR TRANSITION!

Get ready for the next 5 steps to your successful transition. At the end of each Step, I will give simple action points to implement.

ENCOURAGEMENT

Whenever, you are feeling discouraged, I want you to pick up this book and take heart. Whenever you feel like quitting from the looks and expectations of others concerning your hair, I want you to remember that you are not alone. You are not the first to do this and you do have someone in your corner. I am here to guide, inspire and re-energise you as you continue. Some days, you'll be flying high, others running or walking and in between those you may struggle to crawl through this transitioning journey.

I will give you this one proviso:

THERE ARE NO GUARANTEES IN LIFE
AND ONE SIZE DOES NOT FIT ALL.

This is why I have given suggestions for building a regular hair care routine. I have also tried to make them somewhat flexible by adding tips and tricks, which you may find work better for you.

You do not have to do absolutely everything mentioned in this book. And yet, you can still have a smoother transition to natural hair. You will hopefully learn to roll with the changes you notice as your hair grows out. And it will prepare you for dealing with your natural hair.

Just take it one day at a time and you will reach your goal, by God's grace.

STEP 1
HOW LONG IS YOUR TRANSITION?

How long do you plan to grow out your natural hair for? The reason I am starting with this question is because there is no point trying to transition without an end (goal) in sight.

After all:

"IF YOU FAIL TO PLAN, THEN YOU PLAN TO FAIL." HARVEY MACKAY.

Therefore, I advise you to *decide early on* how long you want your transition to be. Will you be embarking on a short-term or long term transition? Here's how to tell the difference:

Generally, a *short term transition* tends to last less than 12 months. If it is longer than a year, it is considered a *long-term transition*. At 12 months, you should have around 6 inches of new growth (natural hair) above your relaxed ends.

I advise that you set a minimum target of 6 months. Personally, I set my target for 2 years. I hoped to have a length of natural hair that I could easily style – say in a bun. I was aware that many women set goals for their transition and then had *a sudden urge to chop it all off* and be natural *immediately*.

As it turned out, I went beyond this target - by 8 months. Why? I was on auto-pilot by then and the transition was no longer hard work for me. I had a quick and easy routine and I could carry on the other important things in my life without my hair suffering for it. Another reason was that I saw another lady on Fotki who grew her hair to tail-bone length before cutting off her relaxer. She showed that I could gauge my hair's growth potential by the combined natural and relaxed length from my transitioning time!

If you fall short of your goal, that's ok – you'll be natural! If you surpass your goal, it's all good. You are still taking care of your hair in transition.

THINKING OF RELAXING YOUR HAIR AGAIN?

This week, someone gave a very good piece of advice for those who are thinking of relaxing their hair again: *just go natural and see how it feels*. Cut off the remaining relaxed ends and wear that natural hair! Even if you only do so for a couple of weeks! The odds are that your new hair will surprise and captivate you.

If not, you can go back to relaxing your hair. At least now you know it is YOUR style of choice. The transition is meant to be a bridge to your future hair, whether relaxed or natural!

DISPELLING THE MYTHS #1: I HAVE TO WEAR AN AFRO ALL THE TIME!

This myth could also be voiced as "there are not that many styling options for a natural with MY hair type". It could not be further from the truth! However, some fear this very strongly. Especially when aiming to cut off their relaxed hair after six months!

With six months of new growth, you have approximately three inches of natural hair to work with. If you choose to cut off the hair to this length, it can be a very sharp contrast to the shoulder-length (or longer) relaxed hair you have just parted with. Your ears are exposed and you no longer have swinging hair! And then you factor in the *shrinkage factor* – the ability of natural hair to appear a lot shorter than it really is because it curls up on itself.

I have seen many naturals, however, who cut their hair at this point and still styled it in very feminine ways. Never underestimate the effectiveness of a cute hairband, a flower and some big earrings. Furthermore, three inches of hair can be styled into braided or twisted styles. These could equally be the main style, or the preparation for another style – say a 'twist-out'. Stretching the hair - elongating the curl pattern - in these styles will display the actual length of the hair.

....

YOUR TRANSITION IS THE TIME TO PRACTISE SUCH STYLES

....

Remember, your transition is the time to practice such styles whilst using the added length of your relaxed ends. I managed to improve my flat twisting technique during my transition. Believe me, it was a long, arduous process trying to train my seemingly auto-pilot braiding hands!

CHOOSING THE LENGTH OF YOUR TRANSITION

Like most things, this is a personal choice. You may decide to do a big-chop before your original chosen date or you might even extend it further. As mentioned above, I extended my date a couple of times before I went ahead with the final chop.

I suggest that you go online today and find a few new naturals or transitioners who have 6 months' worth of hair growth since their last relaxer. YouTube is a good place to start! Videos and photos showing hair growth ranging from 1 year to 2 years are ready sources of inspiration. Which do you prefer - manageability or length?

Many women relish the ease of styling a short crop of natural hair, also known as a *Teeny Weeny Afro* or *TWA*. They simply *'rinse, moisturise and go'* most mornings – wash and go days. Detangling is a breeze and they can try the occasional twisted or braided style.

....

WHICH DO YOU PREFER – MANAGEABILITY OR LENGTH?

....

With length, you could get more *'hang-time'* – the hair is weighed down by its' ends and shows more of its' actual length. However, you have more hairs to detangle and you have to be extra careful with shed hairs knotting along the longer hairs. Over the time it took to grow this hair, however, you would have devised ways of carefully avoiding the major pitfalls (see chapter 3).

So it's really all your choice: do you want to accumulate length, or have a fresh-slate of short hair to work with?

HOW WILL YOU MARK REACHING YOUR GOAL?

Once you've decided how long to transition, I suggest that you set a few interim hairstyling goals for your hair. This way, you can check that *you are still on track and you can encourage yourself.* I advise that you choose a hairstyle you would *love* to try out at *six months* and *one-year post-relaxer.* I chose flat-twists! Initially, I wanted to see whether my hair was looking thicker in this style as my transition lengthened. Secondly, it gave me time to practice and perfect the style.

PICK A STYLE TO WEAR RIGHT AFTER YOU BIG CHOP!

There are so many styles to choose from. To avoid duplication, you can look these up in the *transitioning style manual in step 4.*

Your post-chop style will feel LIKE A REWARD. You could even pamper yourself by getting your hair done at the salon!

GETTING TO KNOW YOUR HAIR!

I went natural after realised I preferred the thicker hair I achieved with less frequent chemical processes. I was also curious to see just what my hair type was! I had guessed it was a 4A/4B mix - I was right - but I had no idea what it would actually look like on me.

I also wanted to achieve those full, fluffy twists I'd seen on YouTubers with similar hair types. I wondered if my hair would shrink up on contact with water – even a deluge of water can't keep my hair from shrinking upwards now! How would my natural hair react to products my relaxed hair loved? How would it react to certain product ingredients – glycerine, proteins, shea butter?

....

'I WAS CURIOUS TO SEE JUST WHAT MY HAIR TYPE WAS!'

....

Not sure what your hair type is? Here is a quick breakdown for you (overleaf):

HAIR SCIENCE I: HAIR TYPES

Andre Walker - Oprah Winfrey's hairstylist - developed a very popular hair typing system. It defined a spectrum from straight to wavy and curly to kinky hair types.

The different hair types are depicted below:

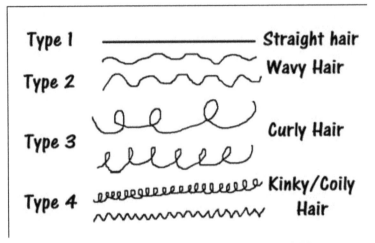

FIGURE 2: VARIOUS HAIR TYPES ACCORDING TO
THE ANDRE WALKER TYPING SYSTEM

TYPE 1 / STRAIGHT HAIR

As the name suggests, this hair hangs straight down – looking smooth and sleek. It tends to be shiny when healthy and may look lacklustre when damaged. As it is bone-straight, the sebum (waxy-oil made by the scalp) makes it way down easily so the hair can feel greasy and weighed down quickly.

TYPE 2 / WAVY HAIR

With its loose "S" curl pattern, this type ranges from 2A (fine), 2B (medium-thickness strands) to 2C (thicker strands) with the last being easy to transform from shiny straight to plump curly styles.

TYPE 3 / CURLY HAIR

Most often likened to a spring, this hair type is tricky to get straightened. Ranging from 3A (looser curl) to 3B (tighter curls) and 3C (tight, almost kinky-looking curls) classification holds.

TYPE 4 / COILY TO KINKY HAIR

Widely seen as the most versatile hair type, these can be styled easily without the needing products like gels. Though coarser and thicker-looking than other hair types, the strands can be quite fine - due to having fewer cuticle layers. In this subtype are: Types 4A ("S" shaped tight coils), 4B (zig-zag kinks) and 4C (pencil-lead thin coils).

Of note, types 3 and 4 hairs can shrink to less than half of their true length – as they are able to absorb water to reveal their true curl potential. They also don't reflect light as well as types 1 and 2 so they have a sheen appearance in stretched-out (straighter) styles.

There are OTHER hair typing systems out there – the LOIS method and the Curly Girl method - to name a couple - but I find this is the one is least fraught with confusing terminology. That being said, read on.

DOES HAIR TYPE MATTER?

The answer is both "Yes" and "No".

Yes, because the way your hair curls affects how well it allows sebum to coat its length. The curlier/kinkier it is, the drier it gets. That will help you to decide on the importance of conditioning and moisture for you. Secondly, you will know how to achieve certain styles on your hair type by observing ladies with similar hair types to you. Their particular tips and tricks will be of immense value – often saving hours of trial-and-error.

However, I also say *No*, because there is more to hair than its degree of curl. One of these factors is *Porosity*. Porosity describes *how easily hair strands absorb and/or lose water*. The less damaged the cuticle (outer layer) of your strands, the lower its porosity. This is a two-way street: if you regularly use heat or colour, your hair will leak water as easily as it grabs it. If you refrain from these practices, you will find you hair takes a while to let water (or moisturizers) sink into it. You have to apply some product, wait a minute, then feel the strand. If it still feels hard, apply a bit more product. Your hair will hold onto this moisture rather well once it's in! Secondly, the thickness of your individual hair strands may be different in spite of having the same curl pattern. One 4a may have thicker strands (medium sized) whilst another has fine (thin) strands. The 4a with the thicker hair may be able to use heat-styling techniques on a fairly regular basis without suffering heat damage (permanently denatured curls) whilst the fine-stranded 4a would get damage after only 1 or 2 attempts.

Hence, if you copy another natural woman's hair care routine EXACTLY, you will not get their EXACT results. This is due to factors like porosity and prior styling techniques coming into play.

BEWARE OF HAIR TYPE ENVY!

Hair types are often an avenue for distraction and discouragement. Why? Two sisters (same parentage) could be transitioning together but find that they have very different hair types. Furthermore, one head of hair can house more than one hair type.

Hair type is determined by the type of follicle your hair grows out of. In straight European and Asian heads of hair, the follicle is round – almost a perfect circle. On wavy and curly heads of hair, the follicle is oval or semi-oval. On kinky heads of hair, the follicle is a flattened oval. Owing to the shape of the follicle, the hair strand comes out in a curving manner and looks spring-like as it twists and turns. The bonds within the strand itself also reinforce this springy shape.

Each head of hair is unique in that the hair type mix per head can vary even in the same family. However, there can be enough similarities to allow you know you can try out certain hair styles if someone else has managed it.

The sad truth is that some people embark on their journey to natural hair with hopes of having a very different hair type from what they see at their roots. They hope that once the chemically–processed portion is removed, they will have looser curls!

FIND THE BEAUTY IN YOUR HAIR!

I advise that you examine your feelings towards your hair and see if you harbour any of these unrealistic expectations. They can set you back before you've gotten very far in the journey.

Instead, find the beauty in your hair: get excited about your new growth! Take pictures as the weeks go by. Count the time post-relaxer until your 6-month post-relaxer. It makes you realise just how far you've come already.

GET INSPIRED!

On this journey, you need every ounce of inspiration you can find! I advise that you go online and search for pictures of ladies with big, natural hair and those with different styles done on similar hair types to yours (suspected). Then, print these off and put them up in your room. Here are some suggested places for finding these gems of inspiration.

- *TUMBLR*: a blog style picture and video sharing site.
- *INSTAGRAM*: an instant upload site for pictures of the day. Love this!

- *FOTKI*: a photo-sharing website with women sharing details of their hair journeys and showing their styles along the way.
- *HAIRLISTA.COM* and *KISS.COM* (keep it simple sista): social networking sites. Basically, Facebook for hair! They also have groups dedicated to transitioners and big-choppers.
- *BLOGS*: there are so many out there with transitioning and natural journeys on display.

You will find a host of ladies (and gentlemen) who are discovering their natural tresses on the sites listed above. If all else fails, a Google image search will yield something for your perusal. I have purposefully omitted Facebook, Twitter and YouTube because it is so easy to get lost on these sites amidst the vast numbers of beautiful heads of hair. I want to give you resources that will help you find what you are looking for in a focussed manner.

In the Appendix section, you will find details of my pages on the above sites so you can use these as a spring-board for finding other inspiration. My friends on these sites are women who inspired and supported me in my transitioning and now natural journey. Enjoy!

See you in Step 2!

STEP 1 – LEARNING POINTS

- **Start Now!** No better time than the present.
- **Get inspired:** go online and print off at least 3 pictures of women with hair types or length you ultimately want to achieve on your natural journey. Push the boat out and think of the long game – is it a shoulder length shrunken wash and go (see transitioning style manual) or waist-length stretched hair?
- **Know why you are transitioning:** do it for yourself.

STEP 1 - ACTION PLAN

- Buy an empty A5 notebook and label it your TRANSITIONING DIARY. Write down your timescale for completing your transition: 6 months, 1 year, 18 months or 2 years.
- Take a few pictures of your hair as it is now: relaxed length check and a picture of the roots of your hair.
- Put up your inspiring pictures: next to your mirror; inside your wardrobe door; and next to a door frame you regularly pass. Why? Seeing them daily will spur on your efforts.
- Now write down your short-term goal hairstyle: Twists in a bun, anyone?

STEP 2
HANDLING THE TWO TEXTURES!

Welcome to the second and possibly the most crucial lesson in your transitioning journey: learning to handle two *very different textures* of hair on your head.

The first texture you will be somewhat familiar with: *your relaxed hair*. Usually, you've had years to get to know this hair, though this doesn't guarantee that you're an expert on it - I know I wasn't! You will have combed through and styled it countless times. Your hairdresser was your go-to for retouch treatments (relaxer applied to your new growth every 1-2 months) and you would get a trim when told to. I'll raise my hand to the fact that I only truly understood my relaxed hair in the year-and-a-half prior to my decision to go natural. Before that, I had no "healthy hair care practices" to speak of.

....

"IT'S TIME TO EMBRACE THE NATURAL!"

....

The second texture is *your new growth* or *natural hair*. You've always slightly dreaded its appearance whilst waiting for the next relaxer touch-up. You've been known to straighten it to blend it in with the relaxed hair. And of course, you are mystified by this hair! It seems to have a mind of its own and feels very different to the rest of your hair. At this point, that thinking is over – it's time to embrace the natural!

In this chapter, you'll learn two important things:

1. Protein is your hair's best helper!

2. Gentle detangling and handling of your hair will reap huge benefits!

MY RELAXED HAIR HABITS

When I was relaxed, I went to the salon whenever I took out a protective style like braids (with extensions) or a weave. When I shampooed my hair, it felt like war! I deep conditioned my hair a handful of times. Yes, for almost 2 decades I only deep conditioned a handful of times! Sadly, I also had burns on my scalp from relaxer treatments left on too long – in spite of my protests in the salon chair!

Style-wise, I wore a ponytail like there was no tomorrow. I say 'ponytail' but it certainly didn't swing in the wind! I would blow-dry my hair weekly (or more often) and put it back in the ponytail. Funnily enough, I never really saw the connection between my blow-drying habits and the short hairs (my ends) on the bathroom floor!

Lastly, I avoided getting a trim *like it was the plague*! This was because of experiences with scissor-happy hairdressers throughout my youth.

Needless to say, I had flat, lifeless-looking hair for most of my life, which hovered between my collar bones and just past my shoulders. And between us, I always felt somewhat bald-looking after a fresh relaxer treatment.

BE KIND TO BOTH TEXTURES

You have decided to transition. You will find yourself getting excited seeing your new growth at the roots. You'll marvel at the curling, coiling and kinking of this hair. You love the feel of it and even take selfies (self-portraits) of your roots – I kid you not, this is a real thing! You're probably tempted to take a picture now if you haven't already! After all, you only have to hang onto those relaxed ends whilst babying the roots, right? Stop. This thinking is flawed. For your transition to be successful - or less frustrating - you need to be kind to *both* textures.

DISPELLING THE MYTHS #2:
"YOUR HAIR WILL BREAK AS YOU TRANSITION"

After I decided to grow out my relaxer, I went online for inspiration. I found out that I was not alone in this fear. Many women had been told much the same: "your hair will handle the transitioning process". *Most women are told they have to cut or shave off their hair.* Can you guess where most of this advice was dished out?

Yes, at hair salons! This is understandable, given that natural hair was initially a *fad* that only a few die-hard women held to. For many, the main reason for going natural was *hair loss from chemical processes*. In these cases, they often had more than a small patch of hair loss that could be hidden. A friend from University told me that as most of her hair broke off after her first relaxer and she decided NEVER AGAIN. I can't say that I blame her.

> *'MOST WOMEN ARE TOLD THEY*
> *HAVE TO SHAVE THEIR HAIR.'*

Whilst at University, I heard at least two other similar stories where women who had been relaxed for many years *had one very bad experience and lost most of their hair*! They went natural in a heartbeat. Given that nightmare situation, I would have to! This was not my personal experience though.

After I joined online hair care communities, I found that many women had managed to grow out their hair for more than a two-year transition. Without cutting their hair at the start! When they did cut their relaxed ends off, they had healthy, thick natural hair at a length they could style. This was enough proof for me! I started planning my transition. From these ladies, I learned some secrets for growing your hair without one texture suffering whilst the other thrived. This was where I learned about the *demarcation line*!

Definition:
The *demarcation line* is the point where the new growth or natural hair ends and the relaxed or chemically-processed hair starts. This is a point where both textures continue in a line with each other. Hence, *it is the most fragile part of the growing hair strand.*

HAIR SCIENCE II: RELAXERS WEAKEN THE HAIR STRAND

During chemical treatments like relaxers, texturizers or perms, the disulphide bonds (strongest bonds helping to keep the hair's shape and texture) are broken whilst the hair strand is stretched and straightened. The end results are hair strands that are devoid of kinks or curls.

As a key component of the disulphide bonds, Cysteine is used as a marker of the intrinsic strength in a hair strand. Amino acid analysis of relaxed hair have shown significantly reduced Cysteine levels in them when compared to natural hair strands.(Khumalo et al. 2010)[1] These lower levels imply fragile, brittle hair. More recently, it has also been shown that the force required to break a chemically-treated hair strand was much lower than for natural hair. Additionally, the relaxed hair strands were less elastic than natural hair. (Bryant et al. 2012)[2]

Given the above facts, relaxed hair is easier to break off, especially if they are mishandled during the transition. In contrast, natural hair still has its inbuilt elasticity and strength to withstand breakage (breaking of hair when combed or styled). This highlights the importance of being gentle with the demarcation line. Whilst transitioning you need to avoid placing undue stress on the strands as this could literally snap off the relaxed ends of the hair.

FIRST LESSON: PROTECT THAT DEMARCATION LINE!

Given the different strengths of the new growth and the relaxed hair below it, one needs to proceed with caution during the transition. This is not a hard to do. On the contrary, the solution is quite simple: *strengthen both the relaxed hair and the demarcation line* with protein treatments.

Before I expand on this, I want to underline the difference between *Breakage* - hair breaking along the length of its shaft, usually at the ends - and *Shedding*. Shedding is a natural process, which up to 15% of one's hair strands are doing daily. This is approximately 100 – 200 hairs! Breakage is not natural! Whilst shed hairs have a white hair bulb - the root - attached to them, broken hairs do not. After shedding, the hair follicle prepares to start another growing cycle.

SHEDDING IS A NATURAL PROCESS. BREAKAGE IS NOT!

Broken hairs are still within the hair growth cycle. They account for the ends of the hair strands. Hence, they are usually shorter in length than most of your hairs. Breakage also usually occurs due to dryness, weakness or mishandling of the hair.

BREAKAGE ALERTS YOU TO A BAD HAIR CARE PRACTISE!

Protein treatments attempt to address the strength issues within the hair. One important thing to note is this: *breakage is how your hair alerts you to a bad hair care practise*!

WHAT ARE PROTEIN TREATMENTS?

Protein treatments usually contain plant-based or synthetic proteins or amino acids - protein building blocks. These are often attached to water molecules – hydrolysed - to allow them to better penetrate the hair strands.

When applied to damp or wet hair and left on for at least 15 minutes, these proteins can slip into weaker areas of the hair strand and temporarily help reinforce the hair strands. These treatments strengthen the hair strands by infuse them with building proteins. Using a gentle source of heat helps these treatments to have their effect quicker – heat makes the cuticles of the hair open up to allow the active ingredients to sink into the hair strands.

....

FOR A TRANSITIONER,
PROTEIN TREATMENTS ARE A MUST!

....

Please note, they cannot reverse the damage done by relaxers and other chemical treatments. Once the disulphide bonds in the hair strands are broken, they cannot be reformed!

However, protein treatments can bolster the intrinsic strength of the previously damaged strands. Therefore, protein treatments are a must for a transitioner!

TYPES OF PROTEIN TREATMENTS

Protein treatments are generally classified into one of three categories: light, medium-strength and strong. Light protein treatments can be used weekly. Medium ones are used less frequently, usually every 2 to 4 weeks whilst strong treatments are used once every 6 to 8 weeks or less.

Deciphering which category a protein treatment falls into can be quite challenging. I advise researching each on hair care forums for further clarity. Nonetheless, at the end of the chapter, there will be examples of each category of protein treatment. The choice of which strength will be based on the degree of damage you are trying to recover from.

For instance, moderate to strong protein treatments are usually reserved for hair that is experiencing excessive breakage - the lightest handling leads to many broken hairs. I advise initially trying a medium-strength protein treatment and seeing if this solves the problem before moving up in strength.

When searching for a protein treatment – also known as *protein-based deep conditioners (DC)*– look for clues in the name. These include terms like *"Reconstructor", "reconstructive", "fortifying", "strengthening", "replenishing", "nourishing", "protein", "mayonnaise"* and *"breakage-control"*.

HOW TO APPLY A PROTEIN TREATMENT?

A protein treatment should be a part of your regular wash day – a day you've set aside a few hours for washing, conditioning and styling your hair. It can be applied before or after you shampoo your hair. The former is known as a PRE-SHAMPOO CONDITIONING TREATMENT OR PRE-POO - SEE *STEP 3* FOR MORE ON THIS!

You should always follow a protein treatment with a moisturizing deep condition. The only time you don't need to do this is if your chosen protein treatment is a light protein conditioner with some moisturizing properties. For medium or strong protein treatments, however, you must deep condition after. The latter - usually labelled as *RECONSTRUCTORS* - often have guidance or instructions provided by the manufacturer for their safe and proper usage. Please follow the specified timing guidelines for these treatments.

ALWAYS FOLLOW A PROTEIN TREATMENT WITH A MOISTURIZING DEEP CONDITION.

REQUIRED TOOLS: Protein treatment or conditioner, 4-8 sectioning clips, a plastic cap and your indirect heat source such as a table-top hood dryer, blow dryer with a hood attachment, steamer or steaming cap, or a hot damp towel.

A) HOW TO | DO A PRE-POO:

- Divide your hair into 4-8 sections depending on your hair's length and thickness – more sections as hair gets thicker and longer.

- Rinse your hair with warm water, towel or t-shirt dry it to dampness and apply your protein treatment in sections. Braid/twist/clip up each section.

- Cover your hair with a plastic cap and sit beneath your chosen heat source for 15-30 minutes (or as instructed on the bottle). *If using a steamer, you don't need a plastic cap - just a towel to protect shoulders from condensing steam.

- Rinse your hair well with warm water and apply your shampoo. Continue with your wash routine (see Transitioning *step 3*).

A) HOW TO |PROTEIN TREATMENT AFTER SHAMPOOING:

- Rinse the shampoo from your hair and squeeze out the excess water with your hands.

- Apply the protein treatment to your hair in sections and braid/twist/clip away each completed section.

- Cover your hair with a plastic cap and sit beneath heat source for 15 – 30 minutes (or as instructed on the bottle).

- Rinse hair well with warm water and squeeze out excess water.

- Apply your moisturizing deep conditioner and continue with your wash routine (see Transitioning *step 3*).

HAIR STORY II - MY EARLY TRANSITIONING MONTHS

I grasped the importance of protein early on in my transition. I had already noticed the benefits to my hair when I used them in the two weeks before and after my relaxer touch-ups. My hair was smoother, felt stronger and my ends did not break off. These all resulted in my having longer hair. I reasoned that this would have similar effects for my transition and my guess was correct!

As my hair approached the middle of my back, I knew that I would have to continue these efforts to keep the length during my transition. I researched different protein treatments – they are not all equal – and chose which ones to use regularly. I will share the products I used and how often I used them at the end of the chapter.

Please remember, protein is not a magical formula which permits poor haircare practises. There are several other important ways to keep your demarcation line strong during your transition – see *Handling the Demarcation line.*

TWO VERY DIFFERENT TEXTURES

You will find that your natural hair behaves increasingly differently to your relaxed hair as you continue your transition. This is entirely normal.

QUICK SIDE-NOTE:

If you began your transitioning journey with long hair - past Armpit length (see glossary at end of book) - *learning to gently detangle your hair is a MUST!* If you don't learn this important lesson by six months' post-relaxer, you will suffer from breakage and likely lose the length you were trying to hold onto.

'GIVE YOUR NATURAL HAIR WHAT IT WANTS'

The main difference between both textures is that *your natural hair requires more moisture* than your relaxed hair ever did. To remedy this, *give your natural hair what it wants*. After all, at the end of the transition, you will be cutting off the relaxed hair. You don't want to discover dry, fragile natural at that point. Hence, by giving your new growth moisture, you are investing in your future hair.

Conversely, you must take steps to prevent your relaxed hair from feeling too stretchy and weak - signs of being over-moisturised.

Below are a few tips to keep the balance:

- I strongly recommend that you continue with protein treatments before each moisturising deep conditioning session. This will keep your relaxed hair strong yet supple.

- Add coconut oil when moisturizing your hair. This oil sinks into the hair and binds to the proteins, preventing weakness. It also prevents *hydral fatigue* – the swelling and expanding of hair every time it is in contact with water. Thereby, it will stop your relaxed hair from absorbing too much water.

- Finally, you must learn how to detangle and comb through your hair gently.

HANDLING THE DEMARCATION LINE

- **Use the correct tools:** a wide-toothed comb or detangling brush is essential. Please, do not even look at a fine-tooth or regular-spaced comb at detangling time. The wider the teeth, the less likely you are to snag your curly new growth and break hairs. Additionally, the relaxed hairs tend to stick together below your new growth – especially when wet. A wide tooth comb will lift and separate these with minimal to no breakage.

- **Detangle with care:** At the start of your transition, detangling will be a breeze. You have probably gone for longer without chemical touch-ups before. However, as the time since your last relaxer lengthens, so will your detangling time. *Please be patient.* Never start detangling your hair when you only have 10 minutes to spare. Rather, put your hair up - in a bun, for instance - and come back when you have more time. (See below for more tips).

- **Wet hair is very fragile:** Water stretches your hair, making it smoother and straighter. However, it will seem to be more elastic that it really is. As mentioned above, the relaxed ends will also stick to each other. In light of this, I advise washing your hair in twisted or braided sections if it is shoulder-length or longer. Secondly, I advise initially detangling before or after washing it - not during. Damp hair is moisturized enough not to break easily. If you are a long-term transitioner, you will find that from 12-18 months, in-shower detangling may become a better option for you. At this point, you have enough natural hair to suit this detangling technique.

- **Do not try to blend your natural hair into your relaxed ends:** You are going natural. Therefore, you should refrain from trying to hide your natural texture. What I mean is that you should avoid using heat- styling tools to straighten your natural roots to look like the relaxed length. The problem with this approach is that you will end up weakening your natural hair by creating heat-induced wear and tear. If this continues, the hair you will have at the end of your transition will not resemble your natural hair – instead it will be *heat-damaged hair*! Use heat sparingly, if at all - for special occasions only.

- **Blend your relaxed ends to your natural hair:** For how to do this, please see the Transitioners' Style Manual in *step 4.*

- **Use a leave-in conditioner after washing your hair:** this will allow your hair to remain smoother as it dries – even without using heat. I used protein-based leave-in conditioners (mainly, Organics Leave-in Liquid Hair Mayonnaise) for the first 12 months of my transition and it made all the difference with styling.

DETANGLING YOUR TRANSITIONING HAIR

Here are my tried-and-tested tips for detangling your hair:

- **Always start with moisturized hair:** Detangling on dry hair is a recipe for disaster.

- **Use a detangler or moisturizing conditioner with slip:** *Slip* is *how well a comb glides through your hair when you add a given product.* In some products, the key ingredient is a silicone. Natural equivalents include Olive Squalene, Coconut oil and Aloe vera juice.

- **Take your time:** Don't rush to detangle your hair. As your hair grows, you will need more time to detangle it. The same is true when you are fully natural.

- **Work in manageable sections:** Don't try to detangle half or even a quarter of your head, especially if your hair is full of tangles. Divide each section in half and if it is still difficult, divide again.

- **Invest in a good comb or finger-detangle:** this is a wide-toothed comb, preferably seamless. As you get longer natural hair at your roots, you can experiment with detangling brushes - like the Denman Brush and Tangle Teezer. *Finger detangling is a labour of love!*

- **Start from the ends of your hair:** Hold the hair just above the portion you are combing through and comb downwards. It will prevent undue strain on the demarcation line above. Tease out each tangle then move higher to comb out further tangles. Patience is the key!

- **Have a spray bottle handy:** Fill it with water or a water-based mixture. This way, if some sections become dry, you can refresh them and continue detangling.

Well, that's all one needs to know about the Demarcation line, protein treatments and detangling hair in transition. Here are the promised protein treatments suggestions - both store-bought and home-made.

SUGGESTED PROTEIN TREATMENTS

KEY: * Products I have used.

LIGHT PROTEIN

*VITALE OLIVE OIL HAIR MAYONNAISE
*ORGANIC ROOT STIMULATOR (NOW ORS) REPLENISHING PAK CONDITIONER
CRÈME OF NATURE CONDITIONING RECONSTRUCTOR
*MOTIONS CPR PROTEIN RECONSTRUCTOR
*MANE N TAIL ORIGINAL CONDITIONER
*LEKAIR CHOLESTEROL PLUS
*AFRICA'S BEST ORGANICS HAIR MAYONNAISE
ELASTA QP FORTIFYING CONDITIONER
*APHOGEE 2 MIN RECONSTRUCTOR
*AUBREY ORGANICS GPB GLYCOGEN PROTEIN BALANCING CONDITIONER
TIGI CATWALK OATMEAL AND HONEY CONDITIONER

MEDIUM PROTEIN

*ORS HAIR MAYONNAISE
MOTIONS MOISTURE SILK PROTEIN CONDITIONER
*JOICO K-PAK DEEP PENETRATING RECONSTRUCTOR
DESIGN ESSENTIALS 6 N 1 RECONSTRUCTIVE CONDITIONER

STRONG (HEAVY) PROTEIN

VITALE RECONSTRUCTOR (MEDIUM/HEAVY)
*AFFIRM 5IN1 RECONSTRUCTOR (MEDIUM/HEAVY)
APHOGEE 2-STEP PROTEIN TREATMENT (HEAVY)
NEXXUS EMERGENCEE (HEAVY)
NEXXUS KERAPHIX (HEAVY)
MIZANI KERAFUSE (HEAVY)

THE TRANSITIONER'S HANDBOOK | 25

PROTEIN-BASED LEAVE-IN CONDITIONERS

*INFUSIUM 23 ORIGINAL (DILUTED 1 PART TO 6 WITH WATER)
*APHOGEE GREEN TEA RECONSTRUCTERIZER
CANTU SHEA BUTTER LEAVE-IN CONDITIONING REPAIR CRÈME
*CHI KERATIN MIST
*MANE N TAIL ORIGINAL CONDITIONER
*AFRICA'S PRIDE ORGANICS LEAVE-IN LIQUID HAIR MAYONNAISE

DIY PROTEIN TREATMENTS

- **Simple Protein Deep Conditioner**
  * Start with a cheap conditioner like VO5 or Herbal Essences.
  * Add 1-2 eggs (depending on hair length) and 2 tablespoons of honey- a natural humectant.
  * Apply to hair and leave on for 20-30 minutes under a plastic cap or bag.
  * Rinse and shampoo out.
  * Follow with a moisturizing conditioner for at least 5-10 minutes.
  * DO NOT APPLY HEAT (you don't want cooked eggs in your hair).
- **Avocado and Egg Conditioner**
  * Take one soft avocado, and mush it up into a paste.
  * Add an entire egg, and beat it until creamy.
  * Rub the mixture over the hair and scalp, and wrap in plastic.
  * It can be tough to rinse (use warm not hot water) but it's so worth the effort!
  *FYI: Avocados contain vitamin B6 & vitamin E
- **Avocado Deep Conditioner**
  * Ingredients: 1 small jar of mayonnaise (a few tablespoons) and 1/2 an avocado
  * Peel avocado and remove pit and mash it up in a medium-sized bowl.
  * Add the mayonnaise with your hands until it's a consistent green colour.
  * Smooth into hair and cover with a plastic cap or bag. Leave on hair for 20 minutes.
  * For deeper conditioning, wrap a hot damp towel around your head over the plastic cap.
  * Store any extra mixture in refrigerator and use up within 1 to 2 weeks.
- **Coconut Honey Deep Conditioner**
  * Ingredients: 4 tablespoons of Coconut oil and 2 tablespoons of Natural honey.
  * Put the coconut oil and honey in a small plastic bag.

* Place it in a cup of hot water for 1 minute to warm.
* Apply to hair and cover with a plastic cap.
* Wrap hair in a towel for 20 minutes. Wash and dry your hair.

STEP 2 - LEARNING POINTS

• The demarcation line is the most fragile point in your hair strand – very prone to breaking.

• Breakage is not a natural thing - it is often how your hair alerts you to a problem: dryness, weakness or mishandling!

• Protein treatments help to strengthen both the demarcation line and the relaxed ends. You must choose these with care.

• Learning to gently detangle your hair is a MUST for protecting the Demarcation line.

STEP 2 - ACTION PLAN

• Choose a protein treatment and plan a day to try it out.

• Follow the instructions for applying a protein treatment.

• Document how your hair feels immediately after rinsing it and after it dried.

• Plan your next treatment day (in the following week or two) and again document your findings. Your hair should feel stronger and smoother as you continue.

STEP 3
GET A GOOD TRANSITIONING REGIMEN!

Your hair care regimen is the handful of techniques you routinely carry out with the aim of growing healthier hair. This is an important foundation for your natural hair. With a good routine, you will be able to grow and enjoy your natural hair with relative ease. It is as crucial as choosing what hair styles to wear! (See the 'Style manual' chapter). It will also enable you to create said styles without as much of a headache – figuratively speaking – as is often encountered as the transition lengthens. To know your hair is half the battle. To give it what it needs are the basics of your hair care regime.

Before we launch into the building-blocks of your transitioning routine, let's tackle another popular natural hair myth.

DISPELLING THE MYTH #3: "I CAN'T GO NATURAL, IT'S TOO EXPENSIVE!"

There has been this long-held belief that natural hair is not an affordable hair grooming choice. This seems to be perpetuated by the plethora of 'Natural' hair care products which are significantly more expensive than those aimed for chemically-treated tresses. I remember hearing certain product prices and thinking, "No way!" with a sinking feeling.

However, I have learned three things which debunked this myth:

1. **Not every expensive product is filled with amazing ingredients** – sometimes you are simply paying for the brand name and packaging!

2. **Get to know your product ingredients** - then you can pick more affordable or generic brand products that are just as effective as the higher-priced ones. This takes practice but I advise you to look at the back of the bottle and spot the similarities between conditioners which make your hair smile!

3. **Homemade hair care is just as good!** I started making homemade deep conditioners and masks from things in my kitchen. The key ingredients were often cheaper than buying a similar finished product. YouTube is also full of tutorials with demonstrations for usage of your homemade products. Be careful when storing these: most water-containing concoctions are only good for 1 or 2 weeks in the fridge – they can grow worrying microbes after this time (without an added preservative).

A great resource is a book by Crystal Swain-Bates, *"How to go Natural without going Broke"*.

Once you have a better idea of what ingredients work for you, you can start to buy more luxurious hair products. I suggest that you initially INVEST IN SAMPLE SIZES for the sake of your purse. For more tips on 'not breaking the bank' – see Step 5.

BUILD YOUR TRANSITIONING ROUTINE - THREE PARTS

A basic hair care routine consists of four parts: *Washing, Conditioning, Moisturizing* and *Sealing*. These steps are usually repeated on a weekly basis or as frequently as your hair style requires. Now let's begin with hair washing.

1. WASHING TRANSITIONING HAIR

A clean scalp is the basis for healthy hair growth – hair grows at its optimum rate. Furthermore, you should aim to start all new styles on clean hair. When free of dirt and product build-up, hair is less prone to tangling (and breaking) whilst you manipulate it. Finally, you need to know how to manage your hair in its most fragile state: when it is wet. To avoid breaking and excessive tangling whilst washing your hair is this: *avoid washing your hair when it is loose.* A few braided or twisted sections will infinitely ease the process.

The most pertinent decision for your wash day is your CHOICE OF CLEANSER. Shampoos are not the only products available for this purpose. With the recent push towards more "natural" and "sulphate-free" shampoos and cleansers, it is crucial to understand the benefits of each available cleanser. I will outline the categories of cleansers and give a list of some you can choose from. Cleansers fall into four groups: *shampoos, non-sulphate cleansers, rinses* and *cleansing clays.*

SHAMPOOS:

Shampoo comes from the Indian word *'Champu'* which involved massaging the head and hair, usually with fragrant oils. The addition of washing hair with soap came with European hair cleansing.

Traditional shampoos - available since the turn of the 20th-century - are based on saponified liquid soaps. Saponification involves a chemical reaction between coconut oil and sodium hydroxide to create sodium lauryl/laureth sulphate (SLS) containing soaps. The first SLS-shampoos were quite similar to the detergents used for washing clothes. Hence, they often proved too harsh for hair – especially curly and kinky hair types which tend to towards dryness naturally (see daily moisture section for why this is). They also caused a rise in the pH of the hair strands causing the cuticles (outer layer of the hair) to stand up and the hair strands to tangle up in each other. Hence, hair is more prone to being broken whilst shampooing the hair.

Now, there are milder cleansing agents (surfactants) which are used in combination with SLS ingredients. However, quite a few women with curly and kinky hair have found that they were unable to continue using SLS-containing shampoos due to its' drying effects. Nonetheless, these shampoos *can* be used to clean the hair whilst ensuring your transitioning hair is not dried out. You must carefully choose your shampoos. Those labelled "moisturizing" tend to be creamier in consistency and thereby reduce the stripping of the natural oils.

HOW-TO | SLS-CONTAINING SHAMPOOS ON TRANSITIONING HAIR

- **Start with wet hair.** This reduces the amount of shampoo you need as it spreads more easily over wet hair. It also reduces the number of rinses you require as it lathers quicker.
- **Shampoo your hair in sections.** Braid or twist up the hair into two or four sections before wetting it and applying shampoo.
- **Try diluting your shampoo.** You can start with 50/50 dilutions. I advise that you always pour it into another bottle or bowl before adding water (for the preservative to remain effective).
- **First apply the shampoo to your scalp** and massage with your fingers.
- **Rinse the shampoo down the length of your hair.** This is usually enough to clean the strands. Shampoo is primarily used to clean the scalp.
- **Repeat once more only if needed** – it is more drying with each application.

SULPHATE-FREE CLEANSERS

Owing to the aforementioned harshness of sulphate cleansers, sulphate-free alternatives were developed. Additionally, there are non-shampoo options also available for cleansing the hair.

SULPHATE-FREE SHAMPOOS

These have been developed with milder surfactants – the ingredients which help to clean the hair. They are still shampoos and will lather up easily during the wash session.

CLEANSING CONDITIONERS

These, as their names imply, are conditioners formulated with added surfactants to allow them to clean your hair. They are also mild with the added bonus of moisturizing the hair. These are not to be confused with 2-in-1 shampoo and conditioners as the later have often have sulphates and are not very mild.

CONDITIONER-ONLY WASHING (CO-WASHING)

This is different from using a conditioning cleanser. This involves using a regular instant conditioner to wash your hair. This works because conditioner has some surfactant in it which can clean the hair whilst it continues moisturizing the hair – its' primary purpose. To clean the scalp, gentle massage with the pads of your fingers before rinsing out the conditioner.

HAIR RINSES

APPLE CIDER VINEGAR RINSES

Apple Cider Vinegar (ACV) not only removes dirt and product build-up from hair but also restores its optimal pH balance –to between 4.0 and 5.0 – thereby sealing the cuticle, smoothing the strands and easing tangles. To use, simply mix one-part ACV with 4 – 6 parts of warm water and apply to your hair. Do be careful to avoid your eyes (it can sting) whilst you gently massage your scalp with the pads of your fingers. This can be done between washes on its' own, or as the final rinse after cleansing and conditioning your hair. Don't worry! The vinegar smell quickly evaporates as your hair dries!

BAKING SODA RINSES

Baking soda is a great clarifier! It can remove product build-up which regular shampoos and conditioners often cannot remove, to give you light-weight, clean hair. To use, add 1 tablespoon of baking soda to 500-800mls of warm water and mix well before pouring it over your hair. Alternatively, you can add the baking soda to a cupful of your instant conditioner (outside the bottle). Stir well – you will see the conditioner become more liquid – and apply to your hair from root to tip. Massage your scalp gently then rinse. As baking soda is alkaline, you need to restore your hair's pH balance by following with an apple cider vinegar rinse to smooth down the cuticles.

CLEANSING CLAYS

Over the last 2 years, clays have risen in popularity as alternative methods for washing the hair. As they often have clarifying and moisturising properties, this is not surprising. The two clays I will mention here are Rhassoul and Bentonite Clay.

RHASSOUL CLAY

This clay used for detoxifying, purifying and conditioning skin and hair. It is mined from the Atlas Mountains of Morocco or from lakeside deposits, sun-dried and micronized (powdered). There are claims that it has been used for over 1,400 years by nobility in Ancient Rome and Egypt.

It consists of Silica (58%), Magnesium (25.2%), Aluminium (2.47%), Iron (0.64%), Sodium- (2.3%) and Calcium (2.34%). On mining, it is a brown polished soap-like rock, but is micronised to a silken, smoother texture. This makes it a light gray colour. It is smetic (swells when water is added) and becomes a smooth paste with water added. When used, it can help to improves skin elasticity, clarity and firmness, removes dead skin cells and surface oil on skin. For hair, it cleanses the strands whilst leaving it moisturised and easier to detangle.

How I used this clay:

- Mix 60g (4 tablespoons) of clay with lukewarm water to form a paste. Use more if needed – I regularly used this on waist length hair and had some spare for a facial).
- Apply to your hair in sections, starting from the roots to the tips.
- Cover your hair with a shower cap and leave in for 20-30 minutes.
- Wash out the clay thoroughly with warm water.
- Optional: You can add 30mls of Aloe vera juice or honey to this mix (for extra moisturizing properties).

I found this clay made my hair soft and easy to detangle from root to tip. As I rinsed each section, I was able to finger-detangle the hair. The added bonus of this clay is that you only need a little amount to cover a lot of hair. This is because it swells up after adding water.

BENTONITE CLAY

Purported to attract dirt and toxins, this clay often used on hair as an alternative to shampoo and on the face as a purifying facial! It has also been used as an intestinal detoxifying agent around the world for centuries. Bentonite clay is rich in Silica (61.4%), Aluminium (18.1%), Iron (3.5%), Sodium (2.3%) and Magnesium (1.7%) with trace amounts of Calcium, Titanium and Potassium. This odourless powder has a creamy grey colour with a very fine, velvety texture.

How I use this clay:

- Put 100g of Bentonite Clay mix into a non-metallic bowl (metal will react with the clay). *I had mid-back length hair when I last used this recipe. If your hair is longer or shorter, you will need more or less.
- Add Apple Cider Vinegar in small amounts and stir to mix. It should form a paste-like consistency. It will be lumpy at this point!
- Stir 30mls of Aloe vera juice into the mix - this makes it smoother.
- Apply to your hair in sections and cover with a plastic cap for 20-30 minutes. Then rinse well.

You will find that the clay weighs down your hair as you apply it. On rinsing, my hair felt squeaky clean but still soft. I found that I could rinse my hair loose and not have a head full of tangles. Lastly, I did not need to follow up this clarifying wash with a conditioner. I advise spraying each section of your hair with water before applying the clay and not to allow the clay to dry in your hair (harder rinse-out).

2. DEEP CONDITIONING FOR TRANSITIONERS

This is a MUST for every transitioner as it will stand you in good stead for your natural journey. Our hair is dry by nature (see *Hair Science* below for explanation). Hence, it needs regular infusions of moisture to soften the hair. Conditioning also helps the hair to dry quicker and be styled with greater ease - owing to a smoothed down cuticle layer. Before discussing more benefits and how to deep condition your hair, I will briefly explain why kinky and curly hair types tend to be drier than their straighter counterparts.

HAIR SCIENCE III: WHY DOES NATURAL HAIR GET SO DRY?

Hair of African descent grows from a flat, elliptical (curved) follicle and exhibits varying degrees of kink and curl. The degree of curl is genetically pre-determined though it is not uncommon to have very different textures seen between same-parent siblings. Hair texture and thickness may also change over the course of one's lifetime. Hence, to a point, *your hair texture is unique to you.*

The curved shape of the strands is at the root of the predisposition to dry hair. In the scalp, each hair follicle is connected to a sebaceous gland, which produces **sebum**, an oily-waxy substance full of fatty acids aimed at nourishing the hair strand and preventing moisture loss. Moisture loss in hair strands leads to splitting of the hair at its' driest parts- the ends. Split ends produce an area of weakness in the strand, which can easily be overcome (or broken) during daily manipulation – combing, washing and even rubbing against clothes.

Split ends can also widen and split further up the length of the hair before breaking off, thereby sabotaging hair growth efforts.

In straighter hair textures, this sebum easily travels down the length of the hair and is why these individuals often feel their hair is 'greasy'. In curly textures, the sebum has a harder time travelling down the hair strands over the bends and twists of the hair. The tighter the curl or kink, the harder this process becomes, allowing moisture to be lost relatively quickly. Knowing that curly-kinky hair has a tendency to dryness emphasises the importance of regularly replacing this lost moisture.

<u>Definition:</u>

A **deep conditioner** is a product designed to be *left on for longer* than an instant conditioner – from 20 minutes to an hour. Whilst instant conditioners only work on the cuticle layer, these *penetrate deeper into the hair,* thereby allowing absorption of its' moisturizing ingredients. An indirect heat source can be used to aid this process as the heat raises the cuticles, allowing ingredients to move inwards faster. Examples of indirect heat sources include hood dryer, conditioning cap, steamers and damp hot towels.

FIGURE 3: CONDITIONER IN TRANSITIONING HAIR - AFTER 2+ YEARS

WHEN AND HOW TO USE A DEEP CONDITIONER?

A deep conditioner is used either immediately before or after washing your hair. Below are my suggested steps:

1. Start with wet or damp hair that is parted into 2-4 sections.
2. Apply a palm-full of conditioner to one section, starting with the ends of your hair, and then apply to the roots and smooth down the hair.
3. Twist or braid up this hair to keep it separate. If it starts to loosen, divide it in half and braid each one.
4. Repeat steps 2 and 3 on the remaining sections.
5. Cover your hair with a plastic cap and either:
   a) With heat: Cover your head with a conditioning cap, a hood dryer or a hood attachment for a blow dryer for 20 – 30 minutes. These are indirect/ safe heat sources.
   b) Without heat: leave the cap on for 45 minutes to 1 hour whilst doing chores. You can cover this with a hat if going outdoors.
6. Remove the plastic cap and rinse your hair (in twists or braids) very well with warm water.
7. Gently towel - or t-shirt -dry your hair to until it is damp and therefore, ready to style.

THE BENEFITS OF DEEP CONDITIONING FOR TRANSITIONERS

These are manifold:

- Smoother, softer hair.
- The ends of your hair - the oldest parts - will not dry out so quickly.
- Hair is less prone to forming new split ends.
- Hair is easier to style when moisturized hair than dry or static-filled.
- Your hair is less likely to break at the demarcation line.

This list is by no means exhaustive. Try deep conditioning weekly or up to monthly on your transition. It will make a world of difference to your hair's feel, health and growth. Take your time to experiment with both homemade and store-bought conditioners.

3. DAILY MOISTURIZING FOR TRANSITIONERS

Having a daily plan for keeping your hair supple is one of the best things you can do for your transitioning hair! Whether chemically straightened or natural, curly/kinky hair tends to dryness. The reasons for this were explained in the *Hair Science* section above.

Hence, it is important to re-moisturise curly/kinky hair regularly. Additionally, you need to apply oil and smooth it down the strands to mimic the function of sebum. This is known as *'Sealing'* – locking in the moisture for longer.

Establishing a daily routine is not hard. However, I must stress that **one size does not fit all**! By this I mean, you still need to pay attention to the other factors affecting how well-hydrated your hair is. Factors like cold winds, rain, snow, heated rooms, woolly clothing and changes in the humidity levels all influence the success of your moisturizing efforts. You will learn to tweak the basic routines to achieve the optimal amount of moisture as your hair grows out. As a rule of thumb, **moisturize your hair to suit your natural hair**, not the relaxed ends – which you will ultimately cut off anyway!

Here are three interchangeable moisturizing methods to tweak on your transitioning journey:

A. THE WET-SET METHOD

This works for blending the straight/relaxed ends of your hair with the curly/kinky natural roots. Therefore, it is a routine for setting your hair in a curly style. You can also use your moisturizing routine to re-set the hair every 2 to 4 days. In between, you can lightly spray with water (See *the Spray and Go method* but avoid dampness or you will lose the set effect).

1. Divide your clean or freshly-washed hair into 4-8 sections and secure with clips.
2. Pour a dime-size of your chosen moisturising lotion or cream into your palm and rub both palms together.
3. Gently apply this to one section, starting halfway down the length of your hair to the ends. Apply more product starting at the section (see "Appendix" for natural oil suggestions).
4. Braid or twist up the moisturized section and set the style using rollers, perm-rods, pin-curls or Bantu knots.
5. Repeat these steps on the remaining sections.
6. Cover your hair with a satin scarf or bonnet at night to prevent loss of moisture overnight.

B. THE SPRAY AND GO METHOD

This is for when your hair is hidden in a protective style. These can vary from a bun to box braids or a weaved style. Although you can take down a bun and use the other two methods, I have found that I could use this method and still retain length.

This ensures that your hair does not become so dry within a style that it breaks off when you take it down. Please don't use with the "out of sight, out of mind" approach. This usually ends with "out of hair"!

1. Fill a clean spray bottle with your chosen moisture mix. This could be water, water and aloe vera juice, or a diluted moisturising conditioner. For a while, I used water and Infusium 23 leave-in every few days - this mini-protein treatment felt wonderful!
2. Divide your hair into 4 sections and begin spraying one section lightly from the root down. Proceed down the hair's length.
3. With braids, you can dip a clean sponge in a small amount of your spray solution (in a small bowl), squeeze out the excess and gently squeeze the remainder into the braids from the top to the bottom of each section.

4. If you are wearing a sew-in weave or crochet braids, simply lift the extension hair out of the way whilst spraying the braid. Move along the braids and across the rows.
5. Once you have completed one section, repeat on the remainder.
6. Use a towel or t-shirt to gently squeeze off any excess water (in case you were heavy-handed).
7. At bed-time, cover hair with a satin scarf or bonnet to keep your style looking fresh.
8. If you have a curly hair set, mist the hair lightly - you can spray above your head and it will land on your curls - then gently tuck the hair inside a satin bonnet for bedtime.

C. THE L.O.C. METHOD

This is for natural hair that craves moisture - a routine for very dry hair. This hair may have been worn loose for a while – a few days to a week. An example would be a week-old braid-out that you are ready to style differently but need to moisturize well beforehand.

To tame the beast (forgive the pun), I recommend the L.O.C.– Liquid-Oil-Cream (or butter) Method. Some women have reported that they could go a couple of days without re-moisturizing after using this method. That has not my personal experience though!

1. Start by lightly misting the hair using a spray bottle filled with water or your chosen moisturizing mix.
2. Separate hair into 4-8 sections and secure with sectioning clips.
3. Gently detangle one section using a wide-toothed comb. If difficult, apply a lotion-type detangler or moisturizer.
4. Once detangled, apply an oil like coconut, jojoba or olive oil (different oils and their properties are listed at the end of the chapter).
5. Finally apply a dime to a quarter-sized (5-penny to 2-penny) amount of a creamy leave-in conditioner, hair balm or butter and smooth down the section.
6. Braid or twist up the section and complete the rest of the hair.
7. At night, cover your hair with a satin scarf and/or bonnet.

HOW YOUR MOISTURE ROUTINE FITS INTO DAILY LIFE?

I recommend doing your moisturizing routine once or twice a day. I do this as I check my hairstyle before leaving for work daily. These routines can take as little as five minutes and less if your hair is already styled. With small efforts, your transitioning hair will be less likely to break or misbehave during styling sessions. You will also learn how your natural hair reacts to different moisturizing ingredients – a very important lesson!

RECOMMENDED HAIR CLEANSERS

SHAMPOOS:
Crème of Nature (red and green label) Shampoo,
Design Essentials Moisture Retention Conditioning Shampoo
Aubrey Organics Honeysuckle Rose Moisturising Shampoo
Elasta QP Crème Conditioning Shampoo

SULPHATE-FREE CLEANSERS:
Moisturizing Sulphate-free Cream Shampoo by Queen of Kinks, Curls & Coils
BeUnique Bamboo Monoi Milk, Gentle Hair Cleanser

CLAYS:
Rhassoul Clay
Bentonite Clay

RECOMMENDED CONDITIONERS

MOISTURE-RICH INSTANT CONDITIONERS

- *TRESemmé Naturals Vibrantly Smooth Conditioner*
- *Herbal Essences Hello Hydration Conditioner*
- *Schwarzkopf Supersoft Repair & Care Conditioner* – with Shea Butter & Coconut-Extract

- *Queen of Kinks, Curls & Coils* Pre-poo Detangler & Nourishing Conditioner
- *Shea Moisture Coconut & Hibiscus Curl & Shine Conditioner*
- *Aussie Miracle Moist Conditioner* – with Australian Macadamia Nut
- *Aussie Mega-Instant Conditioner* – with Australian Kangaroo Paw Flower Extract
- *Aussie Colour Mate Conditioner* – with Australian Wild Peach Extract
- *Giovanni Tea Tree Triple Treat Conditioner*
- *Giovanni Smooth as Silk Deeper Moisture Conditioner*
- *Giovanni 50:50 Balanced Hair Remoisturizer Conditioner*
- *Hair One Cleanser and Conditioner* - with Olive Oil for Dry Hair

MOISTURIZING DEEP CONDITIONERS

- *ORS Olive Oil Replenishing Conditioner*
- *Keracare Humecto Creme Conditioner*
- *Nexxus Humectress Ultimate Moisturizing Conditioner*
- *Elasta QP DPR-11+ Deep Penetrating Remoisturizing Conditioner*

D-I-Y DEEP CONDITIONING RECIPES

HONEY & OLIVE OIL HAIR MASK
1. Mix 1/2 cup honey and 3 tablespoons olive oil.
2. Work a small amount at a time through hair until coated.
3. Cover hair with a shower cap; leave on 30 minutes.
4. Shampoo well and rinse

JOJOBA HAIR CONDITIONER
1. Ingredients: 1 cup rose floral water, 1 tablespoon jojoba oil and 10 drops vitamin E oil.
2. In the top of a double boiler, gently warm the rose water.
3. Once rose water is warm, add jojoba oil. For extra conditioning, leave on for several minutes.
4. Rinse thoroughly with warm water. Shampoo and rinse again with cool water.

COCONUT HONEY DEEP CONDITIONER
1. Ingredients: 4 tablespoons of Coconut oil and 2 tablespoons of Natural honey.
2. Place coconut oil and honey in a small plastic bag and place it in a hot cup of water for 1 minute to warm.
3. Apply to hair, wrap hair in a towel for 20 minutes.
4. Wash then dry hair.

FINAL WORD ON STEP 3:

Don't be afraid to change things up!

As my hair grew out, my routine changed. It was inevitable. Every 6 months, I had to change my wash routine and my detangling method.

For instance, I initially exclusively detangled on damp, freshly washed hair. By 18 months in, I detangled in the shower. Personally, I never could detangle on dry hair and still cannot! In my wash routine, I used to apply my protein treatment or moisturizing deep conditioner and leave it on overnight. In the morning, I would shampoo and follow with an instant moisturizing conditioner. After 6 months, I cut out shampoos and co-washed mainly. At the two-year point, I had added in clay treatments and apple cider vinegar rinses for clarifying my hair. I also used more at home conditioning mixes later in my transition.

If your fail-safe is no longer working, try a different method.

STEP 3 - LEARNING POINTS

- You will need to change up your hair care regimen as your hair grows out.
- Only make small changes at a time: one new thing a week. Review the effects of these changes over at least 4 weeks.
- Choosing a non-drying cleanser is very important.
- Always follow a shampoo or cleanser with a moisturizing deep condition.
- Gently detangling your hair will stand you in good stead for your natural journey.

STEP 3 - ACTION PLAN

- Choose your shampoo or cleanser and designate a day to wash your hair: also known as Wash Day.
- Invest in a good deep conditioner (or try a homemade recipe).
- Allow your hair to air-dry after applying a moisturizing leave-in conditioner.
- Detangle and style your hair - *note the ease with which you do this*.
- Note the change in the feel and manageability of your hair with a good moisturizing hair wash routine.

STEP 4
STYLE IT - LIKE A PRO!

Most people rush into choosing a transitioning style. Many believe that there is only one they can wear: namely, braids with extensions.

When I first encountered new naturals, most recounted tales of wearing braids throughout their transition. It seemed like *everyone* wore braids or weaves for their whole transition! That always struck me as odd. You see, I believed the transition was a time to start *enjoying natural hair styles* and hopefully *perfecting them*!

Of course, I wasn't too surprised when their next words were, *"I had no idea what to do with my natural hair once I big chopped!"* How could they? They had never tried styling their own hair!

Let me further clarify: before my transition, I tried doing two-strand twists on my relaxed hair. My hair looked limp with thin ends that unravelled easily (see picture overleaf on the left). I was planning to finish with a perm-rod set - to resemble corkscrew curls - but I don't think I bothered in the end. At least my hair looked shiny. I like to focus on the positives!

Two years (8 months into my transition) later, with 1-year's worth of Texlaxed hair above my natural roots, my twists were unrecognisable! (See the picture below on the right.) *FYI: Texlaxing is applying relaxer to the roots of your hair for only a few minutes to achieve thicker hair.* These twists were much thicker and looked more natural – excuse the pun! Sure, the ends were still thin but the length and thickness at the roots more than made up for it.

FIGURE 4: TWO-STRAND TWISTS IN JUNE 2008 (LEFT) VS JULY 2010 (RIGHT)

My point is this: you need to start trying out natural hair styles early in your transition. This way you can see how your hair is changing! As it grows out, it gains texture and volume.

The other reason to try out these styles is this: you can learn which styles flatter your face shape, your head and of course, which earrings go best with each style! Lastly, it gives you a chance to practice and improve on new styling techniques. My personal bug-bear were flat-twists! Now, let's talk about how to execute them. The remainder of this chapter is the *Styling Manual*! These styles are low maintenance in that they allow you to keep your regular regimen going with little fuss in between styling days.

These hair styles are either ***protective styles*** or ***low-manipulation styles***.

PROTECTIVE STYLES

These are simply *styles in which the ends of your hair are hidden within the style and are thus, protected from the elements: Sun, wind, rain and snow.*

Protective styles were my go-to styling preference even before my transition. Most can be maintained for up to two months and allow you to easily care for your growing hair within. These are exemplified by braids or twists with extensions and sewn-in weaves. By the end of my transition, my go-to-styles were flat-twists or two-strand twists in a bun. Before my transition, I could not flat-twist to save my life!

Nonetheless, there is a time and a place for protective styling. I immediately think of the autumn and winter months, when the cold weather, rain and snow can wreak havoc on the hair. At these times of year, wearing fabrics like wool can also be very drying to the hair. And let's not forget the indoor heating!

....

THERE IS A TIME AND A PLACE FOR PROTECTIVE STYLING'

....

Protective styling focuses on the oldest parts of each strand - the ends of your hair. This is because they have been exposed to more daily wear and tear than the rest of the strand. By the time your hair reaches shoulder length, the ends have spent 1-2 years growing away from the scalp. This is two years of being away from the moisturizing sebum of the scalp, whilst being in regular contact with the elements and your clothing. This makes them prone to forming split ends - where the strand splits in two or more pieces.

Split ends also occur with daily activities like combing, washing and styling the hair. Worse still, these split ends can cause breaks higher up the strand, thereby affecting more of the hair's length. In addition, transitioning provides a new point of weakness in the strands – *the demarcation line.* Your main aim during your transition should be to retain the length of the strands by avoiding too much combing and styling.

LOW-MANIPULATION STYLES

As the name implies, *in these styles you leave your hair alone for a while.* This differs from a protective style in that it does not necessarily hide the ends of the hair from the environment. Examples of such styles include braid-outs, twist-outs, bantu-knot outs and curly sets.

These styles allow you to prepare or set your hair and wear a certain style for up to a week without needing to re-braid, re-twist or comb your hair in between. By reducing the frequency of handling, you save those ends from too much wear-and-tear. Thereby, you can retain more length through fewer split ends and broken hairs.

HAIR SCIENCE: WHY IS CURLY/KINKY HAIR SO PRONE TO BREAKAGE?

The basic structure of a hair strand is that it has an inner cortex, surrounded by multiple overlapping layers of cuticle (like roof-shingles). The innermost portion of the strand is the medulla. The cortex gives the hair strand most of its strength, thickness and colour. This is true across all races. However, whilst straight hair appears oval or circular in cross-section, curly or kinky hair is like a flattened ellipse. Additionally, the hairs of those of African descent are tightly coiled.

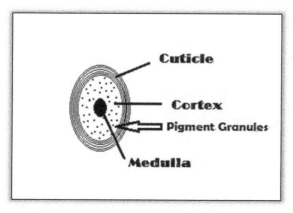

FIGURE 5: PICTURE OF HAIR STRUCTURE.

In a study observing hair strands across three races - Caucasian, Asian and African - by Khumalo *et al.* (2000) it found evidence of wear and tear (loss of the cuticle layers) across all racial groups. Of note, the tightly coiled hairs from subjects of African descent showed *splits along the length of the hair strands* and *multiple complex knots,* which were not seen in the other racial groups. They also noted that most of the hair strand ends were broken. It seemed that many of these splitting points and broken ends were caused by difficult combing sessions, which likely tore at the knots causing the breaks.

The main cause for this higher breakage rate was felt to be due to the coiling pattern of the hair. Every twist and bend in the hair strand is a potential point of weakness which can be overcome during harsh styling sessions. Add to this mix, hairs shedding from the roots. These try to slide down the strands but inevitably get caught up between the other kinks and coils, sometimes forming knots around the hairs still attached to the scalp.

This highlights the need for gentler hair care practices as well as hair styles which prevent excessive combing.

CHOOSING YOUR TRANSITIONING STYLE

Choosing a style at the start of your transition need not be a daunting task!

Before you attempt any new style on your hair you should start by Washing, Conditioning and Detangling your hair. This should be accompanied by a protein treatment to strength the hair throughout the length of the style. For some styles, you may dry your hair completely in another style beforehand - say in braids to lengthen the curls.

The style must be something you can easily care for without causing damage to your growing hair. There is no point installing micro-braids, for instance, if you know you don't have the patience to remove them gently - or to moisturize them daily, for that matter! The same is true of wearing a sew-in weave for so long that you have a dry, matted mess underneath. Any style you do choose must have a *low maintenance routine*! You also need to be able to do a protein and/ or conditioning treatment on your strands at least once a month. This way, you maintain a strong demarcation line and healthy natural roots.

Below is a table with examples of protective and low-manipulation styles, respectively.

PROTECTIVE STYLES	LOW MANIPULATION STYLES
Buns	Braid-out
Single braids with/without extensions	Twist-out
Two-strand Twists / Senegalese twists	Rod sets
Cornrows	Bantu Knot-outs
Flat-twisted styles	Curlformer sets
Weaves	Roller-sets
Wigs and half-wigs	Wash and Go

The rest of this chapter will consist of step-wise instructions for achieving common protective and low-manipulation styles. I won't be attempting to teach you anything too advanced like installing weaves on your own head – for one thing, that needs assistance! I'll just be giving basic styles which you can vary and build on with practice. Now let's start!

PROTECTIVE STYLING MANUAL

EDGE (HAIRLINE) CONTROL

BUNNING 101

PARTING YOUR HAIR

BRAIDED STYLES

TWISTED STYLES

STYLING WITH EXTENSIONS

EDGE (HAIRLINE) CONTROL

I would be remiss to speak of hair styles without mentioning the all-important finishing touch on the EDGES. This refers to the front and side perimeters of your hair where shorter hairs often border the rest of the hair. Another similar area is the KITCHEN AREA - the hair above the nape of your neck.

I am highlighting these areas because even with relaxed hair, these areas of hair would often take on a fly-away look by the end of the day. Sleeping without a satin scarf gave the same result. As your natural texture grows out, this area can form a small halo of natural hair in front of an otherwise sleek style. The kitchen area can also have short curls which hang out from up-do styles and ponytails. Knowing how to gently handle this area will prevent many a headache.

Here are two techniques:

THE GEL-DOWN METHOD

This involves dampening the perimeter of the hair and applying some gel to your hair line to smooth it down in the direction of the style. A silk or satin scarf is then tied over the hair firmly but not tightly, to keep the style in place and allow the gel to dry. The drying can be overnight, over 30 minutes to an hour (if not too much gel is used) or for a few minutes under a hooded dryer.

The end effect is a lovely smooth hairline which shows the wavy texture of the hair but does not frizz up during the day. Most gels work well though some cheaper gels will cause flaking when they dry. Flaxseed gel is a natural gel that can be made at home and works well.

THE SMOOTH/BRUSH DOWN METHOD

This involves using water as your setting lotion and either a soft boar-bristle brush (this has natural fibres and will distribute the sebum well) or your fingers to smooth the hair. Spray water on the edges and use your chosen implement to smooth your hair in the direction of your style. Then cover your hair with a satin scarf firmly (but not too tightly). Allow the hair to dry over 10-20 minutes then remove the scarf. This method can be supplemented with a styling pomade after spraying with water to help it last longer.

These techniques are generally very good but you need to avoid overuse of the brushing technique as *you can cause traction hair loss* with the repetitive action. I simply use my fingers and a scarf for achieving most of my smoother looks.

BUNNING 101

THE BALLERINA BUN | HOW-TO

Also known as the Sock bun, it was the first style I mastered once my hair was past my shoulders. Its very elegance belies the simplicity of achieving this look. It also hides the fact that it could be made using a clean sock! Yes, you can opt to buy a doughnut-shaped bun-insert (in a matching colour to your hair), you can make your own at home!

Skill level: Easy

Hair length: Shoulder length and beyond

Tools: Detangling comb / brush; two Ponytail holders; Bun Insert; and Styling gel or cream.

1. To make your own bun insert, use a clean black sock. Cut the toe portion of the sock off and roll the sock upon itself to form a doughnut shape!

2. Gently gather your moisturised hair it into a ponytail and securing with a ponytail holder. Place the bun insert over the ponytail, pulling the hair through the hole. Gently loosen the ponytail by inserting a finger in front of the ponytail holder and pushing it outwards from the base of the ponytail - you don't want traction hair loss at the edges of your hair.

3. Fan the hair over the sides of the bun and place a second, thinner ponytail holder over the fanned out hair. This will create the shape of the bun.

4. Lift the bun insert and gently tuck the ends of the ponytail underneath the insert.

5. For the edges of your hair, lightly spray with some water and apply a styling gel before covering with a satin or silk scarf. Allow to dry for 5-10 minutes.

Pro Tip!

Make sure you cover the bun insert well with your hair – don't give the game away! If you don't want to use a second ponytail holder, loosely wrap your hair around the bun insert and pin down the ends. (See 1st picture below)

LEFT (VIKA S.) AND RIGHT (MYSELF)

THE HIGH-BUN | HOW-TO

Also known as a "Top-knot Bun", this simple and chic style only takes a couple of minutes to achieve. You can re-invent an older hairstyle with this. You can also turn most low-manipulation styles into this one with just a ponytail holder and a couple of bobby pins!

Skill level: Super-easy

Hair length: Shoulder length and longer

Tools: Detangling comb; Ponytail holder (sturdy); Styling gel/ cream; and Bobby pins.

1. Gather your moisturized hair into a high ponytail either with your hands or using a comb. Secure it with your ponytail holder.

2. Using one hand, twirl the ponytail and wrap it around the base of the ponytail.

3. Pin this bun down around the base using 2 – 4 bobby pins.

4. You can use a styling gel or cream to smooth down the hairs leading into the ponytail and tie it down briefly under a silk or satin scarf for 5 – 10 minutes. This will give an all-day smooth finish!

Pro Tip!

Don't pull make the ponytail too tight or it will give you a headache! The longer your hair is, the more times it will go around the base of the bun. If your hair is not long enough, use a sock insert to make this bun!

THE CHIGNON | HOW-TO

This sleek bun has graced the silver screen worn severally by Grace Kelly and others portraying Royal reserve. It can be worn as is or with a few choice accessories above the bun.

Skill level: Intermediate

Hair length: Just past shoulder length and longer

Tools: Detangling comb / Brush; Styling spray; Ponytail holder; Bobby pins.

1. Start with clean, detangled straightened hair. Create a 1-inch long centre part at the front of your hair, then brush the hair down and gather to the just above the nape of your head.

2. Secure the hair with a ponytail holder an inch or two above the nape of head.

3. Roll the hair downwards over 2 finger and fluff it out to make it look fuller. Pin the bottom of the roll to just below the ponytail holder.

4. Spray your hair and use your fingers to smooth the hair and cover with a silk/satin scarf for 5-10 minutes to allow the style to set.

Pro Tip!

This style has to *look sleek and controlled*. Don't pull the hair too tightly though. You can use the pin-tail end of a pin-tail comb to further fluff up the roll of the bun.

TWISTED BUN / CINNA-BUN | HOW-TO

I love this bun even now on a fully natural head of hair! It takes a bit of work to master but the height of the bun gives it a *crown-like effect*. Fitting, I feel!

Skill level: Intermediate

Hair length: Collar-bone length and longer

Tools: Detangling comb/ Brush; Styling spray or gel (optional); and Bobby pin / Hair pins.

1. Gather your hair into a high ponytail and secure with an Ouchless ponytail holder.

2. Divide the ponytail ends into 2 – 8 sections and loosely two-strand twist each one.

3. Taking one twist at a time, wrap it around the ponytail in one direction and pin the ends down. With each successive twist, wrap in the opposite direction.

4. Once all twists are pinned down, gently tease the middle of the bun with your fingers to hide the ponytail.

5. Apply your styling product to the hairline and use your fingers or a soft boar bristle brush to smooth down your edges. Alternately, cover with a satin/silk scarf for 5-10 minutes.

Pro-Tip!

To maintain this style, cover with a satin or silk scarf folded into a triangle, then tie it at the base of your neck and then once around the base of the bun. To make it a cinnabun, make a wider ponytail base using a larger hair band, then pin-curl and pin down each twisted section.

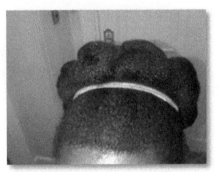

THE FAUX-BUN | HOW-TO

An easy style that mimics an all-natural bun – thanks to the added Kinky straight extensions. You only need hair long enough to be comfortably put in a ponytail (without traction). This style is a suitable for laid-back weekdays *and* sophisticated soirees.

Skill level: Beginner

Hair length: 6 inches and longer

Tools needed: Detangling comb / Brush; 2x Ponytail holders; Black plastic hair bands; Bobby pins; and Styling gel or cream.

1. Start with clean, detangled hair. Gather into a ponytail by hand, securing with a ponytail holder and loosen base of ponytail to prevent traction (push up holder to free edges).

2. Place a ponytail holder over the middle of a single pack of Bulk Kanekalon braiding hair. Loop one end through the middle of the hair bulk and pull taut. Now loosely twist or braid the two halves of the hair bulk and secure the ends with Plastic elastic bands.

3. Place the ponytail holder of the Kanekalon hair over your own ponytail base and fold it two further times to secure.

4. Now begin to wrap the braiding hair around the base of the ponytail, securing it with Bobby pins. Once all wrapped, tuck and pin the ends.

5. Finally, apply your styling gel or cream to the edges of the hair and base of the ponytail and cover with a satin/ silk scarf for 10-15 minutes to smooth and set the hair.

Pro Tip!

As your hair grows, you can use Marley braid or Afro twist bulk hair to achieve curlier-looking buns. To spice things up, mix in a large strand of a lighter colour to the bulk hair before securing with a ponytail holder!

THE FAUX-PONYTAIL | HOW-TO

By all definitions, a ponytail leaves the end of the hair out to face the elements. This is where a Faux-ponytail trumps the status-quo. By applying some extensions (weave tracks or a ready-made ponytail cover), you give the appearance of a ponytail but can hide your own hair underneath it in a hidden bun, braid or twist!

Skill level: Intermediate

Hair length: Long enough to make a ponytail (and have 1-2 inches below it)

Tools: Detangling comb; Soft boar bristle brush; Styling gel; ponytail holder; and hairpins.

1. Start with clean, detangled hair. Gently comb your hair into a ponytail and gather in one hand. Secure the base with a ponytail holder.

2. Braid or twist the hair in the ponytail to prevent tangling, wrap and pin it to the base of the ponytail.

3. Select your weft of hair and pin one end of it to the base of your ponytail. Now wrap it around the base 2 or 3 times, using a bobby-pins to secure as you go. Secure the end of the weft to your ponytail with a last bobby-pin.

4. If using a pre-made ponytail, simply pin it to the sides of your ponytail in 3-4 places to secure it.

5. Apply your styling gel or cream to the perimeter of your hair and either smooth in by hand or with a boar bristle brush. Cover with a silk or satin scarf to set the gel for 5-10 minutes. Remove the scarf to reveal your finished look.

Pro Tip!

Choose a ponytail that is not too heavy or risk putting tension on your edges – traction alopecia is a real concern. Keep it simple: if you have natural roots, choose a curly ponytail. Whilst your roots are still looking straighter (at the start of your transition), choose a straight or wavy ponytail.

CROWN BRAID/TWIST | HOW-TO

The ultimate boho-chic updo that stands alone or can be accentuated with flowers or a headband. This style goes well from night to day and works with your hair in a curly or straightened state –hence, a great transitioning style!

Skill level: Intermediate

Hair length: Collar-bone length and longer

Tools: Detangling comb/ Brush; Styling spray (optional); and Bobby pin / Hair pins.

1. Part your clean, detangled hair the hair in two: either in a centre or off-centre part from front hairline to the nape of your hair.

2. Working one side at a time, begin a Dutch braid or Flat-twist down one side of your hair. Continue braiding along the perimeter of your head, keeping the braid neat.

3. Once at the nape with no more hair to add, braid down to the ends as usual. Repeat on the other side.

4. Pancake the cornrow/ flat-twist – gently pull the outer strands of the braid to make it look fuller. Do this down to the ends of each braid.

5. Finally, cross over the braided ends and bobby pin them to the inside of the opposite cornrows. Use more bobby pins to secure the braid at the middle of the nape.

Pro-Tip!

This looks great with a slanted side-part. You can make it easier by flat-twisting instead od braiding along the perimeter of your hair. Add more bohemian flair by leaving a few tendrils loose above each ear. Below is a Crown-Twist I often wore to work!

PARTING YOUR HAIR

I used to underestimate the importance of parting until I realised just how long sorting the parts out took before creating a new style. Without a doubt, parting the hair is the second most time-consuming element of creating most protective styles. If you don't prepare your hair well before attempting even this step, you could be in for a lot of frustration – and possibly some discomfort from recoiling strands.

Skill level: Beginner to Intermediate (smaller = more advanced)

Hair length: All lengths

Tools: Detangling comb / brush; Pintail comb; Spray bottle with detangler: and sectioning clips.

1. Start with clean, damp hair: if your hair is dry, it will break easily. Spray lightly with a mix of water and your favourite detangling product.

2. Keep the hair in stretched sections until you are ready to part that section. For instance, only take down a few of your large twists to style one part of your head or risk them becoming tangled again.

3. Your sectioning clips will help you keep the hair you have parted separate from the loose hair beside it.

4. Once you are ready to style the parted section, moisturise and seal it with your chosen products before commencing. This will keep your hair in great shape.

Pro-Tip!

Remember, you don't have to have to use a comb to part. The tips of your fingers, pinch-parting are sensitive enough to help you create everything from centre- to box-parts. It takes a bit longer to initially get the hang of it! See overleaf for common parting types.

PARTING TYPES

Centre-part | Front to Back: This allows you to create two-identical styles on either side of your head. Make this part by finding the centre-point of your face and nape, then joining the two points in steps using your pintail's metal tip.

Side-to-Side: This allows you to make demarcate half-up, half-down styles or even just to form a bang area in front. Start by making a part behind each ear, then join them up.

Four-Square Part: Allows you to divide your hair into 4 equal sections. Make this part by combining the centre-part and side-to-side part. You can switch up this part by using the mid-points of each quarter-part to form an X-part line!

Box Parts: These allow you to have neat box-braids and twists. You can form these by hand (pinch off sections with your fingers) or with a pintail comb. For the latter, make a Four-Square Part then make equal rows and boxes within them. You can also stagger each row of boxes to allow the hair to lay flat and "hiding" the parts: the hair in row above fall between the boxes below.

Triangular Parts: Looking striking, these can be made using diagonally divided box parts or by making the first triangles from the mid-point of the X-version of the Four-Square part.

Row Parts: These are great for cornrows or flat-twists. After the four-square part, you can subdivide your hair into lines going towards the back of your head. As you get better, you can make the rows go sideways or in diagonals.

STYLING WITH BRAIDS

SIMPLE BRAID | HOW-TO:

The easiest way to learn to braid is doing it on one large section of hair. Making a basic braid/ plait is simpler when your hair that has been detangled and stretched or straightened. Then as you get better, divide the hair into smaller sections and do it again!

Skill level: Beginner / Easy

Hair length: Shoulder length and longer.

Tools: Detangling comb/ brush; and Hair band.

1. Start with a large clean, detangled section of hair. Separate this into three equal parts or pieces.

2. Cross the section of hair on the right OVER the middle section. Pick up the section on the left and cross it OVER the right (new middle) section.

3. Now take the new piece on the right and cross it over the middle, before crossing the left over the right (new middle).

4. Continue down the length of the hair, bringing the outer sections over the middle to form the braid.

5. To finish the braid, when you have 1-2 inches left, either secure the end with a black hair band or twist to the ends (merge two sections and twist together – see 'How-To' below).

Pro Tip!

Invest in small black plastic hair bands to hold large sections together. Simply cut them when you're taking down the style! As you get better, you will learn to braid down to the very ends by *tapering* the hair (borrow from neighbouring strands as you go down).

DUTCH BRAID | HOW-TO

As this is a step towards cornrowing, I figured I'd throw this style (and the French Braid) in here! Unlike the basic braid (above) the sections cross UNDER the middle piece, to make them stand proud of the rest of the hair. You'll see what I mean below.

Skill Level: Intermediate/ Medium

Hair length: Shoulder length and longer

Tools: Detangling comb/ brush; and Hair band.

1. Start with clean, detangled hair. Take a section near the top of your head and divide it into 3 equal parts or pieces. To start the braid, take the part on the right and cross it UNDER the middle piece, then the left piece UNDER the right (new middle) section.

2. Move the right section under the middle again but add a small piece from the hair below it on the right side.

3. Add a small piece of hair from the left side to the left section before bringing it under the middle. You will be creating a joined-up braid /plait.

4. Continue down the back of your head, adding in equal-sized pieces. Once at the nape of your neck, continue braiding by moving the sections UNDER the middle (the reverse of a basic braid).

5. Tie the end of your braid with a hair band or twist down to the end.

Pro Tip!

This style of braiding tends to remain neater than the French braid (below). That's probably why it forms the basis for the cornrow. It takes practice but it is worth it! In truth, I grew up only aware of the Dutch or reverse method of braiding!

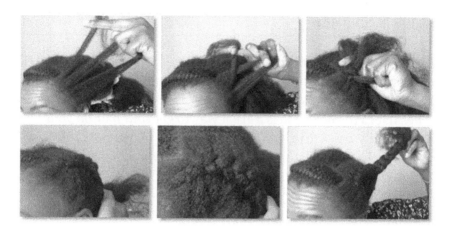

FRENCH BRAID | HOW-TO

Apart from being a very timeless style, this is an essential step towards cornrowing. Whilst the Dutch braid uses a braid-under technique, the French Braid makes the outer pieces cross OVER the middle pieces. It lies flat to the head and is a great way to get your hair off your face. Additionally, you can leave a few wispy pieces of hair out on each side to soften the look! PS: this style works well with straight to curly and kinky hair types!

Skill Level: Intermediate/ Medium

Hair length: Shoulder length and longer

Tools: Detangling comb/brush; and Hair Band.

1. Start with clean, detangled hair. Take a section of hair near the top of your head and divide it into 3 equal parts or pieces. To start the braid, take the piece on the right and cross it OVER the middle piece, then the left piece OVER the right (new middle) section.

2. When you're bringing the right section over the middle again, add a small piece of hair from below it on the same side before crossing it over the middle.

3. On the left, add a small piece of hair from the left side before bringing it over the middle to create the joined-up braid /plait.

4. Continue down the back of your head, adding in equal-sized pieces. Once at the nape of your neck, continue braiding by moving the sections over the middle (a basic braid).

5. Finish the braid by tying the end with a hair band or twist down to the end.

Pro Tip!

You may initially get someone to help you until you get the hang of this braid. As it can be tricky, pay close attention to your non-dominant hand. The direction you're facing matters: look down as you braid for a straight result. Practice makes perfect!

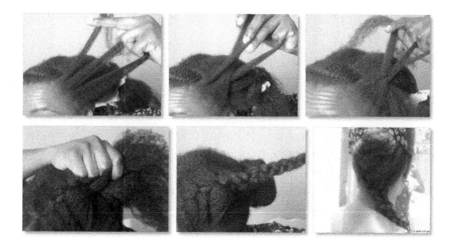

CORNROWING (FLAT BRAIDING) | HOW-TO

Cornrows aka canerows are the ultimate African woman's hairstyle! I would say that though- I have been wearing them since I was a child. They are a basis for so many styles and patterns and you can wear them for 1-4 weeks at a time. They are also the basis for weave styles and crochet braids. The more you practice, the smaller you can braid these!

Skill Level: Intermediate/Medium

Hair length: TWA onwards (you can add extensions if you like)

Tools: Detangling comb/ brush; Pintail comb; spray bottle (detangler); and Sectioning clips.

1. Start with clean, moisturized hair parted into sections and along rows (see Parting section above).

2. Choose the row you want to braid and secure the rest of the hair out of the way with clips. Separate a half-inch of hair near the front hairline and split this in three.

3. Move the right piece UNDER the middle piece and cross them before moving the left piece UNDER the right (new middle) piece and crossing them.

4. As you braid along the row, add small pieces of hair to the right and then the left sections before crossing them under the middle. You're making small Dutch braids.

5. Once you run out of hair to add, finish with a basic braid to the ends.

Pro Tip!

This style takes practice: the main thing is to make neat sections with your parting tool (pin-tail comb). Ensure your hair remains moisturised throughout styling (spray bottle) to save you pulling at knots or tangles. PS: I am still tender-headed so I prefer to do these myself!

TWO-STRAND TWISTING | HOW-TO

Twisted styles are usually kinder to your hairline owing to the lower tension they exert whilst on the hair strands. They also look absolutely gorgeous on well-moisturized hair. I detail how to achieve chunky-sized twists but the sections only need to be divided further to make them smaller, if that is your preference.

Skill level: Intermediate / Moderate

Hair Length: TWA (Tweeny-Weeny Afro) and longer

Tools: Detangling comb / brush; Pintail comb; Spray bottle (detangler); and Sectioning Clips.

1. Start with clean, moisturized hair. Divide the hair into 8 or more sections.

2. Take one section and divide it in two. Start by crossing each section over the other - left-over-right or right-over-left, as you prefer.

3. Continue to do this until you reach the last 1-2 inches of the strands. Try not to borrow hair from the other strand as hair tapers.

4. Repeat these steps on the remaining sections of hair.

Pro Tip!

To make smoother twists, twirl or roll each section in one direction before the twisting them over each other in the same direction. For example, twirling both halves to the right, or clockwise, before twisting right over left. You can twirl the strands between your thumb and index finger. This makes for more-defined twists (and twist outs).

FLAT-TWISTING | HOW-TO

These were personally trickier for me to master but are still quicker than braiding the hair. I had to get to grips with which direction to twist in to make my hair look neater.

Skill level: Intermediate

Hair length: TWA (teeny-weeny afro) or longer

Tools required: Detangling comb or brush; Pin-tail comb; Bobby pins; Elastic hair bands.

1. Start with clean, detangled hair. Part a row of hair using the pin-tail comb – according to your chosen pattern.

2. At the front of the row, make a small section of less than ½ an inch in width. Divide this into two strands and twist the right one OVER the left (or left over right, if you prefer).

3. Add some hair from behind to the new right-hand section and twist both sections right over left again. Repeat this as you proceed down the row, adding hair from the behind.

4. When you reach the end of the row, two-strand twist the hair down to the bottom.

Pro-Tip

This style can be used to create half-up, half-down hairdos. The back portion can then be either more two-strand twists or left loose for different style! When twisting along the hairline, you may find that you have to twist in one direction for the twists to stand proud of the hair.

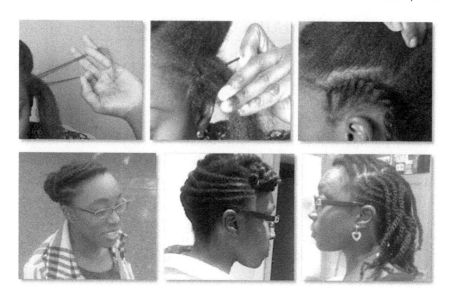

USING EXTENSIONS IN YOUR HAIR

Before you apply any synthetic extension hair to your head, there are some ways to prepare this type of hair to ensure a smoother installation process.

Firstly, the hair will arrive in a large bundle at a very long length. Don't be fooled, one bundle is rarely enough for one adult head of hair! I suggest buying five or six bundles. It is better to have a couple to spare at the end than to run out with one section of your head incomplete.

PREPARING THE SYNTHETIC HAIR

Synthetic hair is treated with an alkaline base prior to packaging. This can cause irritation at the scalp if installed fresh from the pack. To avoid this happening, I advise treating the hair in a shallow basin of diluted vinegar in warm water (1-3 capfuls of vinegar). Leave the hair in this water for 15 minutes before rinsing the bundle, squeezing and hanging it out to dry. I suggest over the side of bathtub or in the shower as it will drip considerably. You can treat several bundles of hair at a time.

After 15 minutes, there will be a thin white film on top of the pool of water: this is the alkaline base from the hair bundle. I suggest doing this at least a day before your planned installation to allow it to fully dry. You can return treated hairs to their original packaging for easy storage.

CUTTING THE EXTENSION HAIR TO YOUR DESIRED LENGTH

For a length to the middle of your back, cut the bundle in half. To prevent wastage, I divide the bundle in two before cutting half of it. That way, I can use the other half for other lengths. To have waist-length hair, fold the hair into three (like you're making an envelope) and cut the last 1/3rd of the hair off. As your hairline in front will fall higher on your back than the nape, I suggest using the 2/3rd (waist) length for the front sections and the ½ (mid-back) length sections from the crown downwards.

SIZING YOUR BRAIDS AND TAPERING THE ENDS

This is mainly according to your particular taste. If you want 'Poetic Justice' or Solange Knowles-style chunky box-braids, you need to pick off larger pieces from your bundle – roughly index-finger thickness. For medium-sized or smaller braids or twists, pick off smaller pieces – roughly half that thickness.

The last step is to ensure that your added pieces will not end in a blunt cut – this doesn't look very natural. To achieve the tapered-ends look (hair naturally grows in a V-shape), you can hold the bundle close to the ends on one side and grab and pull small pieces slightly out of line with the rest of the hair. Another way is to it pull the hairs askew from each piece you have sectioned off before adding to the parted hair you want to braid. Finally, smooth the whole section to remove tangles.

You are now ready to apply the extension hair to your head.

BRAIDING WITH EXTENSIONS | HOW-TO

These are only a step up from braiding your own hair. There are a few different ways to start but I will share the way I have found gives the least tension to your own hair strands. By using your hair as one strand of the braid initially, you don't run the risk of adding too much extension hair and pulling at your roots!

Skill level: Advanced

Hair length: TWA (3 inches) and longer

Tools required: Extension hair; Detangling comb; Pin-tail comb; Sectioning clips.

1. Start on clean, moisturized hair which you've prepared by blow-drying or drying it in large braided sections to stretch it out.

2. Part your hair into 5 large sections: one at the nape (back) of your hair, two sections in the middle (by the ears) and two sections in front.

3. Starting at the back, part a ½ to 1-inch horizontal line from side to side and secure the rest of the hair above it out of the way.

4. At one end, part of a smaller section of ½ an inch width and use a sectioning clip (duck bill clips are good here) to keep the rest of the hair out of the way. Apply a dime (5-penny) size of moisturiser and/or gel to the roots and length of this hair.

5. Prepare your extension hair ensuring that it is the same thickness as your sectioned hair.

6. Holding the extension hair at its mid-point, drape it over your hair section to straddle your hair.

7. Cross your own hair from the middle OVER the synthetic strand on the right. Now cross this new middle strand over to the left.

Continue to cross the middle over the right and then left in a simple braid downwards.

8. At one inch from the end of your own hair's length, borrow half of one of the extension strands and add it to yours. Continue to braid down to the ends.

Pro-Tip!

Sealing the ends: Leaving the tapered ends loose for the last 2 inches, seal them by dipping in hot (just boiled) water for 30 seconds. I prefer to use a mug and go in small sections. For a crimped-ends effect, braid large sections of completed braids (4-6 in total) before dipping in the hot water.

TWISTING WITH EXTENSIONS | HOW-TO

These are much easier and quicker to install than single braids with extensions. You either start with the single braiding technique and start twisting after 1 inch of braiding, or start with a twist (more natural-looking).

Skill level: Advanced

Hair length: TWA (Teeny-Weeny Afro) or longer

Tools required: Extension hair; Detangling comb; Pin-tail comb; Sectioning clips.

1. Start on clean, moisturized hair. Section as you would for braiding with extensions (above).

2. To begin with a braid at the base, drape the extension hair over your section of hair and braid for 3-4 turns (about 1 inch down). At this point, divide one section into two and add them to the remaining two sections before beginning to twist the hair downwards.

3. To begin with a twist at the base, divide your parted section in two and drape the extension hair over these. Combine each half of the extension hair to parts. Roll the synthetic hair and parted hair beneath it between your thumb and index finger in the same direction that you will twist. Once the hairs appear blended, begin to twist the sections over each other.

4. Continue twisting until you are 1-2 inches from the end.

5. Sealing the ends: dip the ends in hot water for 30 seconds to 1 minute. Be careful with the hot water – I use a mug of hot water and dip sections - with a protective towel around my neck.